Code Red

CODE RED

No.1 in Rogue Hackers Series

John MInx

Dark Star Publishing

Contents

CHAPTER 1

The front door bell rang and Jacob Wylde heard his mother move to answer it. There was an exchange of words and then the sound of footsteps coming back inside, entering the downstairs lounge. A low male voice was audible, but nothing of the man's conversation. Instead of trying to listen, Jacob swivelled round in his chair and returned to the computer he'd built himself last year. Although there wasn't a shred of data left on the cutting-edge machine – of that he'd made sure – he still tried running one last scan, almost as an act of superstition. Even though, no matter what they did to the hard drive, nothing recorded on it could link him back to the massive crime. And yet this didn't stop Jacob's heart from pounding furiously as he hoped and prayed the unannounced house call was perfectly innocent.

A false alarm.

Hearing further movement below, he shut the computer down in mid-operation. The door to the lounge opened and then his mother called up to him from the foot of the stairs. "Jacob. You have a visitor." The seriousness of the situation was there in her voice, expressed as naked fear. He had never heard his mother sound that way before and suddenly it became obvious that the worst case scenario was upon him. All he could so was turn in his seat and await that person whose heavy steps he could hear now, getting closer all the time.

It was a man in his forties who entered through the doorway to Jacob's bedroom. 5'10 with thinning blonde hair, dressed for the summer, as if he'd had his holidays cut short and hadn't bothered to change back into work clothes. Immediately the stranger shot Jacob a mean little smile. Despite his casual wear, he was all about the business.

The man stared about him, pulled up the spare desk chair, pushed it over to where Jacob was seated. Then he sat down opposite, so that their knees were almost touching, allowing Jacob a good look of his cold blue eyes.

"Oh Jacob," the man said. "What have you gone and done…"

"Who are you?"

"The name's Wilkins. I belong to government circles but it's you and your crazy antics that have brought me here today."

"That doesn't make any sense," Jacob told him.

"Unfortunately, it makes all the sense in the world. Which is why I thought we might begin with an admission of guilt."

"Really, I don't know what you're on about."

"I'm talking about Project Eames, Jacob. And about your unveiling of this classified prototype to the entire bloody world."

"I thought they'd caught the people who did that."

"All but one. Goes by the nickname RockSteady."

"And you're saying that that's me?"

"It is you, Jacob, and I'm going to ask you to stop with the lies now. Better that we consider your options from here on out. You do actually have a couple of possibilities as things stand."

Jacob looked again at the man's pale blue eyes. They

were unflinching, alert, tempting him to confess. But instead he smiled and shook his head with conviction. "You've made a huge mistake. I think I'd like to talk to a lawyer now."

Wilkins nodded back without it meaning anything. Then he let out a deep loud sigh. "The thing is – you don't get to enjoy it."

"Enjoy what?"

"Dicking us around."

"Like I said, I don't know what you're talking about."

"Yes you do, Jacob. That's the problem. And this thing that you've done means that the usual rules don't apply. You've graduated to the world where anything can happen if and when it's thought necessary. The stakes are ridiculously high and so we get to act like monsters if that's what it takes. My job is to bring this fact home to you. The full significance of what you've done."

"So you're saying I can't see a lawyer?"

"That's the least of it. Let's consider your family for a minute, or should I say your mother, as it amounts to the same thing. Something terrible might be made to happen her, Jacob. That is not impossible if you don't change your tune."

At this Jacob reared up out of his chair and shouted down into the man's face, his voice cutting up rough. "That's not going to happen!"

Wilkins looked up and responded calmly. "No? OK. Fine. Then you need to talk to me openly. We don't have a lot of time here."

Jacob's heart bristled with anger, even as he tried bringing it under control. In the meantime, Wilkins did no more than watch and wait for him to come clean.

"OK. I may have played some part in it," Jacob said finally, lowering himself back onto his seat.

"The thing is, when our own programmers pieced

your escapade together, and read back through all the logs, it seems that your buddies simply did all the donkey work. It was you, almost single-handedly, who achieved the impossible – or what was considered impossible up until a month ago – and penetrated the most forbidding barriers Lockheed Martin have ever erected around their system. This wasn't a case of you simply lending a hand, Jacob. You were the one who made this break-in a reality."

"And what will happen to the others now?"

"Your fellow cyber-terrorists? Oh, they get to be made an example of, plain and simple. Every single one of them is going to end up in jail for the longest time."

"So you have what you want then."

"No, Jacob. Clearly we don't. What we would like, more than anything, is to put the cat back into the bag and withdraw Project Eames from worldwide circulation; but clearly that's impossible now. You have made it so. This was like Christmas and New Year rolled into one for our Chinese friends. Their best people have been working on gaining access to this information for the best of two years, and then you stroll along and hand it to them on a plate, doing supreme damage to the defence capabilities of the United States, and, by extension, ourselves. Billions and billions of pounds will be needed to rectify this mess. Incalculable budgets. And where are we going to find the money? Under your bed?" With this, Wilkins leaned over and lifted up one corner of the quilt as if to check.

Jacob sat there, dazed, staring at the beige coloured carpet between his feet. Finally he looked back up. "So what happens to me now?"

"You actually possess a get out of jail card on account of your god given genius. Enormously unfair, all things considered, but there it is. Obviously, you have a very,

very special gift. And this very special gift permits you to stay away from prison."

"So, what? I come down to London with you?"

"London!" Wilkins laughed. "No, Jacob. Our American partners are insistent that we hand you over to them directly. In fact, they are waiting for you even as we speak, which is why we really must cut these niceties short." With this, Wilkins rose to his feet.

Jacob's hesitation was brief. He felt like he had no option but to comply – given these threats which sounded all too believable – and so he stood up once more, went to the far corner of the room, and made to pick up his Quicksilver day sack.

"No, Jacob. You're taking nothing with you. Not a single possession. You simply vanish into thin air."

"And what if anyone asks my mother where I'm gone?"

"If pushed, she'll tell them that you went down South, got yourself a job, became a productive member of society. I've already explained the options to her. Maybe you could hear that in her voice. She's under no illusions, believe me. The best her only son can hope for is to disappear without a trace."

They left the bedroom, went downstairs, Wilkins leading the way. Jacob's mother was standing there in the hallway beneath them in a state of shock, arms folded tightly across her chest. "The man said that I'll never see you again, love."

"It's early days, Ma. I don't know when, but I promise I'll be in touch."

"Very, very unlikely," Wilkins added, stepping to one side.

His mother moved forward now, took hold of her son and crushed him against her, not wanting to let go. It was left to Wilkins to cut short this goodbye by placing a hand on Jacob's shoulder, explaining that his time was up. As Jacob pulled backwards, he tried fixing his mother with an intense look which would stay with her as a source of comfort. "Please look after yourself, Ma. And remember what I said. Have a little faith."

Together the two of them left by the front door. Outside, the May afternoon had turned overcast with heavy grey clouds moving across a grubby-looking sky. At the end of the short drive, a silver Range Rover Vogue with blacked-out windows was parked up. Wilkins approached the SUV, guiding Jacob by the elbow, and opened the back door to it. Then, with the greatest reluctance, Jacob got in.

CHAPTER 2

"Well, wherever they're sending you to, it can't be much worse than here," added Wilkins as the Range Rover pulled away from the curb, patting Jacob on the knee.

"What would you know?" Jacob replied.

"Actually, I grew up in a similar dump. As for yourself, I understand you could have gone to Cambridge and studied computer science. Had the full scholarship lined up and everything."

Jacob only shrugged.

"Well you certainly dodged a bullet there. Nineteen years of age and still living under your mother's roof. I can see that you've been living the dream instead."

"I make all the money I need."

"Oh yes, with your apps business. What's it called? Tabz? You know, in hindsight, you might have been better off pursuing a future in digital commerce rather than exposing highly classified military secrets for the sheer hell of it."

At this Jacob looked away, out of the window, in an effort to bring their talk to a close.

They skirted Liverpool city centre, came down onto the dock road, and continued along it. Close to the estuary waters, passing old wharfs by. Was he to be placed on a ship? It seemed unlikely, but they were not headed for any airport that Jacob knew of. Instead the journey continued through Litherland and Crosby, keeping near to the coastline, edging Northwards whilst maintaining illegal speeds. The driver up front had no obvious interest in his passengers and never once used the rear view mirror to inspect either one of them, even with Jacob staring often at the man's reflection. Wilkins meanwhile had taken out a Sony Xperia and started tapping away on its keys. Then he lifted the device to his ear and made a terse phone call, keeping to a long string of yes's and no's. As he did so, Jacob watched the scenery go by – dunes, beaches, golf courses – thinking to imprint it on his memory. Some small token of home.

It was only when the RAF airbase came into view, on the vehicle's left, that Jacob had a good idea of where they were headed. Not much further at all. He could remember passing this place one time before, with his father at the wheel of a white Ford Orion, on a day trip to Ainsdale Beach. Back in the mid-nineties. Now his suspicions were confirmed as the Range Rover slowed its speed, turned into the base's drive, and stopped at the main checkpoint. There was a large sign, RAF Woodvale, away to Jacob's right on a freshly cut lawn.

A uniformed guard walked out of the small security post, took papers from the driver's outstretched hand, and studied them in detail. Then he nodded gravely at the writing, returned the documentation. The metal barrier was raised. Wilkins pocketed his phone and turned to face his travel companion. "I'm going to give you one single tip, Jacob. When the man on this plane starts up asking questions, then you should cast your mind back, put your memory at his disposal, and answer him as correctly as you can. Chap by the name of Graves. The fact is they know near enough everything already, but this way they might possibly stop short of shooting you full of drugs or sticking your head down the khazi."

"The khazi?"

"The toilet, Jacob." Wilkins shook his head. "I don't know, the youth of today..."

The base looked like a throwback to an earlier time, with a number of large old fashioned air hangars lined up in a row. But as the Range Rover shot clear of the last of these, making light work of the speed bumps, Jacob caught sight of the plane in question. It lay directly up ahead, perfectly alone. An unmarked, grey Gulfstream V.

The Range Rover approached the plane at speed, crossing the runway tarmac, and then broke smoothly to a stop. "Well Jacob. This is where you get off," Wilkins said.

"Nothing happens to my mother. I have your word on that?"

"Of course. We're not sadists. Simply professionals."

Jacob opened the door for himself, climbed out, heard the ominous sound of the Rolls Royce engines ticking over. He climbed those steps pulled up against the front of the plane. At the midpoint he turned and took one last look backwards at the desolate airfield, as if still trying to find something to hold on to, disorientated by the speed at which his life had changed forever.

CHAPTER 3

At the entrance to the aircraft, in place of stewardesses, Jacob was greeted by two expressionless men in dark blue suits, both six foot plus, a day's stubble on their skulls. No sooner had he stepped on board than one of them moved past him and began securing the door for take-off. The other rapped on that separate door leading to the flight deck and moments later the plane began to reverse around. This second man then gestured for Jacob to move down the single wide aisle, walking closely behind him, until they'd neared a large oval-shaped table with a walnut finish, taking up a third of the available cabin space. There, another man was sat down, reading from a printed dossier with plain blue wraps.

Slightly older than the two agents on the flight, his own suit of clothes was pitch black. He had red hair, expensively groomed, and pale thin lips shut tight. He looked up at Jacob and nodded towards the seat opposite. "Sit down. Buckle up." Jacob noticed that the man possessed distinctive blue eyes also, but unlike those of Wilkins these were darting, restless, brimming with discontent. His voice, by way of contrast, was smooth, belonging to a Southern state. This must be Graves, Jacob thought. The man Wilkins had mentioned. The one he was told he should fear.

Jacob did as asked, lowering himself down into the

black leather chair opposite. He found the two parts of the safety belt and clicked them together.

"Wilkins explained your situation?" Graves asked.

"Basically I'm screwed is what he said."

At this, Graves nodded approvingly. "That's a highly accurate assessment right there."

"I'd love to know what the press would make of all of this," Jacob replied. "Young Man Kidnapped by US Government. Threats Made Against his Family's life."

"I thought Wilkins had been through this with you, Wylde. You don't get to lodge a protest and the newspapers are neither here nor there. That is not part of the deal. The crime you committed grants us license to do as we see fit."

"Different accent, same bullcrap," Jacob muttered.

"Speak up, Wylde."

"Nothing."

"Believe me, the next time you shoot off your mouth, I will have your ass canned, whatever your potential value. There's still a room with your name on it at a maximum security jail of my choosing. I could make that call now and have you transferred there by this evening. Either that or else I'm sure we could squeeze you in at Guatanamo Bay." The man spoke without raising his voice and yet the words hit home. Jacob knew it was time to leave off.

The plane had been taxiing along the runway, now it thrust forwards and upwards into the air, leaving England behind. Graves watched the earth fall away for the best part of a minute, then turned back to confront Jacob. "It seems that you left our best programmers for dead and made a mockery of their latest encryption techniques. In doing that, you've set a new benchmark. The problem is that you now need to remain at that level. Or preferably improve upon it. But falling back is not an option. There can be no future for you unless you continue t prove your worth. Basically your "genius" is ours to use up."

As they reached cruising altitude, one of the agents carried a tray over to the table. It contained a large insulated jug of black coffee. Two cups. Graves poured for Jacob first, filled his cup close to the brim. "Drink up, Wylde. I want you alert. Have about a thousand questions to ask you before we get to where we're going." Then, after filling his own cup to the middle mark, Graves picked up a graphite laptop from the seat next to him. He placed it on the table, opened the lid, and adjusted the screen until satisfied with its exact position. In the back of the laptop, a small red light appeared. Then it shot out a beam which moved up and down Jacob's face repeatedly, as if taking a precise reading from it. At the same time, Graves concentrated on the screen in front of him, typed a word or two via the keyboard, then looked back at Jacob again.

"OK, so when did you first encounter those other members of The DoubleDareCrew?"

CHAPTER 4

It had all begun with a Freeware message board that Jacob used regularly. Here he'd started giving away a few smart little programs of his own devising, mostly for use with Google Android, hoping to direct some traffic to his own website and drum up business for those fee-based apps he was looking to sell on. Mostly platform games for mobile devices. Then, without thinking it through, he'd posted a hack for the latest Sony PSP, demonstrating how to unlock its capabilities and allow for the use of unauthorized software (a breakthrough which had taken Jacob a single weekend to perfect).

The number of downloads this program attracted was soon phenomenal – word spreading like wildfire of its availability – to the point where Jacob sought to distance himself from the illegal procedure by removing it from the site entirely, in an effort to avoid prosecution. And then, a day later, he received an email from someone calling themselves UnPoucoMalouco.

Like your work, RockSteady. Naughty but very nice. How about you join a few like-minds here?

Here turned out to be a private IRC channel called Great/White/Bytes, hosted on a secure server, away from prying eyes. And what Jacob found, on entering this digital arena, was instant understanding among the personalities gathered there. Also, a real appreciation of what he was capable of. The other forum members, six in total, spent two months engaging Jacob in intense shop talk, discussing the various mechanics of computer programming. But at the same time, it seemed to Jacob, they were careful not to say too much or stray onto any highly dubious topics. It was as if they were still checking him out, testing his limits, taking a reading of his character.

Everyone inside of Great/White/Bytes was careful to maintain anonymity, even among themselves, and there was only the quirky use of English to suggest that one or two of them were from foreign speaking parts of the world. However, despite these concealments, a sense of togetherness still flourished on the board and Jacob found that he wanted more of it. For this reason, he decided to take the initiative and perform another hack – this time against the iPhone – before bringing it to their joint attention. Hoping to gain the group's further confidence.

In the aftermath of this bold move, Jacob entered Great/White/Bytes and discovered that none of his online friends were waiting for him there. Instead he found a single weblink in his dialogue box. Clicking on this, the regular architecture of the forum page instantly fell away, to be replaced by the hidden realm which lay beyond it. A clandestine den, superbly encrypted, where the same cast of screen names gathered; only here they schemed with wild abandon and spoke in truth of their outrageous designs.

When Jacob arrived that first time, the others were there already, waiting to congratulate him.

– Welcome aboard, RockSteady. You are now a fully-fledged of The DoubleDare Crew!

– You'll do for me, Rocksteady.

– Me too.

– Ditto.

– Likewise.

– Game on.

In the six months leading up to the Project Eames leak, The DoubleDareCrew's reputation had grown steadily until they were considered among the supreme online hackers' groups, graduating from small-time incursions against modest targets – bombarding websites with DdoS attacks – to elaborate attacks against large institutions, utility companies, major online retailers. Although the crew operated as a showcase for what they could achieve together, there was also a sense of competition among their number as they sought to prove their individual worth. It was through these inner-rivalries that RockSteady soon came to the fore as it became apparent to everybody that his cracking capabilities were second to none. The others could not live with Jacob Wylde, and their growing reputation as a whole was largely due to his astonishing skills.

Time and again, Jacob rose to each challenge and eluded the most elaborate security measures. He was yet to meet his match and his abilities kept on expanding in line with whatever difficulties confronted him. In acknowledging Jacob's greatness, the others encouraged their newest member to make ever more use of it, and, intoxicated by this praise, he felt the desire to play up to this star role and show them exactly what he could do.

The data itself was never the point as far as Jacob was concerned. These were, to his own mind, purely symbolic victories. It was the process itself which bewitched him. The freedom to move around at will. There in his bedroom, Jacob experienced this criminal behaviour as a cutting-edge dream. Blinds closed, headphones on, he found himself inside a perfectly self-contained universe. And increasingly, Jacob became caught up in this sense of unreality which would lead him on to the point of no return.

If there was one topic which obsessed all members of The DoubleDareCrew, then it was Quantica. A fabled US military server, supposedly located at the heart of the Pentagon network. At least that was the widely held belief. It had kept circulating on various forums for years, and every time the rumour threatened to die down completely, there would be a new lead. Word of a sighting. The cyber-version of El Dorado. While heated discussions continued as to whether it was real or only a black-hat myth, the matter was never concluded either way. Now The DoubleDareCrew decided they would be the first to prove its existence for real.

The prime mover in the scheme was Django, the founder member of the group, who claimed to have once caught a glimpse of Quantica's bizarre firewall before being expelled from the Pentagon's operating system. But it was a good moment for a renewed attempt. After all, they had a secret weapon at their disposal.

The mind of Jacob Wylde.

This was how the Lockheed Martin attack first got floated. It was conceived of as a dress rehearsal for the main event, enabling them to perfect their ultimate approach. But when Django suggested this exercise, two of the original seven crew members had called it quits immediately. It was too dangerous an escapade for their liking. Meanwhile the others closed rank, grew tighter. First Lockheed Martin, and then the very heart of The Pentagon. These were the actions which would see The DoubleDareCrew enter the all-time hall of fame.

– You up for this RockSteady? Django wrote. Ready to take on the might of a major defence contractor?

Up till now it seems to me like you've only been pussyfooting around.

– I'll give it a go.

– Good to hear. Looking forward to seeing you in action against a proper heavyweight.

On the fateful evening, the others staged a series of orchestrated dummy attacks on the Lockheed Martin servers to draw attention away from the main assault; leaving RockSteady free for a serious run on the system.

The code he was confronted with intrigued Jacob greatly. The encryption was like nothing he had ever seen, based on incredibly complex algorithms; and yet the more he focused on it, the less forbidding it began to appear. It had the effect, almost, of a hypnotist's watch on his mind – ushering Jacob towards that trance-like state which always signalled his best work. Only this time he went deeper mentally than ever before, as if becoming embedded in the code itself. In this way Jacob started to unravel layer after layer of block ciphers, extracting permission from them as he cut through their streaming protocols. On and on he went, making a nonsense of every encryption in his path, travelling further into the network. His mind boundless, ablaze with calculations, inevitably finding patterns in the code which pointed him in the right direction, as if the programmers had left detailed signposts for the young hacker to follow. It was truly exhilarating. The best feeling in the world. He'd been granted flashes of this vision before, brief glimpses of it, but never anything so sustained.

The minutes speeded by, as did the hours, until Jacob Wylde had arrived at the centre of this covert system, accessing that mother-lode of data long believed to be perfectly secure. In the end, he had not even looked at the chosen file itself, beyond recognising that it featured some kind of schematics. He just wanted to pull something from the record to prove what he had done. And so Jacob extracted Project Eames at random as evidence of his triumph. Then he posted it to the remaining members of The DoubleDareCrew, moments after the event.

Minutes later, Jacob collapsed onto his bed, still fully clothed, and sank into the deepest sleep he'd ever known. For fifteen hours he kept to this semi-comatose state and there was no waking him. His mother tried several times, and it was only when he heard her, distantly, speak of calling in the doctor that Jacob groped awake, told her not bother.

All that next day he was struck with pounding headaches, beyond the aid of paracetamol or aspirin, as if the back of his eyes had been set on fire, torching his brain in turn. After a couple of hours Jacob made the effort to go online – the glare from the screen causing his eyes to water – and this did nothing to ease his pain.

First he saw the top headline on Yahoo News and put two and two together (while straining to pretend that it added up to five). Then he turned to the online newspapers and saw the same trouble writ large. All hell had broken loose on account of Jacob's own actions. That much was clear. The whole world appeared to be running with this story, placing it firmly on page one.

Top Spy Plane Secrets Revealed
Hacker Devastates Lockheed Martin
Military Prototype Published Through Scribd – 'Project Eames'

It was a new airborne surveillance device which Jacob had unearthed: one which made use of a revolutionary propulsion system. And although the file had been pulled from Scribd in a matter of hours, its circulation was still so wide that it had certainly fallen into the wrong hands. Jacob realised that one of his fellow crew members must have put the document up as a way of boasting of their achievements, thus triggering this nightmare scenario.

After taking tremendous precautions, he next tried accessing The DoubleDareCrew site, only to discover that it was already down. There in its place was a bright blue banner which caused his heart to skip any number of beats. It read US Federal Government Crime Scene.

Despite his high fever, Jacob raced to wipe his hard drive clean, conducting a thorough sweep of it. By 9pm that night, according to the newswires, three of the reported five members of The DoubleDareCrew were in police custody. One in Edinburgh. One in Warsaw. Another in Malta. The next morning, according to The Guardian Online, Only a single fugitive remains at large, identified by the authorities as "RockSteady."

CHAPTER 5

Throughout the flight, Graves interrupted Jacob's replies, demanding further clarification on each point. And even then, every complete answer only prompted more questions in turn. The level of detail asked of Jacob was microscopic and in this way several hours passed by. It was only as the plane began its gradual descent that Graves concluded the interview in full. A tray of sandwiches was then brought over to the table and Jacob quickly grabbed one and started wolfing it down. Meanwhile Graves stared at the screen before him. "Any irregularities in your statement," he said, looking the data over, "and you can be pretty sure I'll be back in touch…"

"Well that's how it happened," Jacob answered.

"For your sake, I hope that's true." Graves watched disapprovingly as Jacob forced another sandwich into his mouth. "Quantica doesn't exist, by the way. It's a figment of too many bong hits on the part of your screwy comrades. Now this stupid myth has taken on a life all of its own."

"OK," Jacob answered.

"I can see you don't want to believe me – it must be like giving up on Bigfoot or something – but I can assure you, in this case, it simply isn't true. The Pentagon has no such server to its name."

"I'm not arguing," Jacob added.

Graves closed his computer down. "Shortly you're to meet the one man in the world who has plenty to teach you, as I understand it. And believe me, learning every thing you possibly can from this educator is the best chance you've got of sticking around and retaining a small amount of liberty. Afterwards, if he deems you ready for active duty, then you go to work for us for the rest of your living days."

Jacob said nothing, wondered about his next destination. All the blinds were pulled low over the small oval windows and he had no idea where the jet was about to touch down.

Five minutes later, when the plane had landed and reached a complete stop, Graves nodded over at one of the security detail and the burly man came forward, told Jacob to get up. "It's probably best if you don't ever see me again, from your own point of view," Graves said in conclusion, before returning to his paperwork. Dismissing Jacob completely.

At the front of the plane, the second security agent had already opened the door and was lowering a stepladder. Once this was secure, he told Jacob to walk down it. Jacob complied and before he had reached the bottom, the same man followed on behind.

They had landed on a makeshift runway, with crude markings scored into the earth, surrounded on all sides by tall pine trees. Miles and miles of them as far as Jacob could see. It was late in the afternoon, judging by the sun's position in the cloudless blue sky, but still intensely hot.

A Ford Explorer XLT in black was parked just beyond the shadow of the Gulfstream's wing tip, waiting to carry Jacob away. Now the agent moved ahead of him, reached for the back door of the vehicle, told Jacob to get in. Jacob did so without looking back, although he could hear the plane was already moving away, picking up speed for another lift-off. The agent then closed the back door and climbed up front, next to the driver.

Inside the back of the vehicle, another man was sat waiting. He was in his forties, with a thick head of greying hair, wire framed glasses, a slender nose; dark complexion and a delicate, solemn face. The window next to him was down and he was smoking an unfiltered cigarette whose aroma filled up the 4×4. The man watched with interest as Jacob took a seat and then offered his hand to the new arrival. "I am Professor Farid Radan," he said.

After a moment's hesitation, Jacob took hold of the offered hand. "Jacob Wylde." And with their introductions made, the driver put his foot down and the Ford sped off towards those trees it was already facing.

"I know that for you this is a highly traumatic situation, but for myself, it is a pleasure to meet you and I very much look forward to our working together." Radan had the faintest of accents and spoke English with the kind of accuracy acquired from studying it closely for many years. "Your attack against Lockheed Martin demonstrated an elegance of mind that is impossible to teach. Although this is not to say you have nothing still to learn…" At this, he threw away the butt of his cigarette and closed the window so that a cloud of tobacco smoke remained inside.

"So, what, you teach hacking?"

"In a manner of speaking, among other things. You sound sceptical?"

"I don't know what I'm doing myself half the time. I just do it."

"Of course, of course. This is more about preparing you for those new technologies which are set to become commonplace before too long. We are hoping to give you a head start in this respect. Also we will be analysing the mindset of other programmers, the better to second guess them, and concerning ourselves with probable scenarios. And then I have also thought to include a detailed study of past mathematical models. This is not for the purposes of a rounded education, you must understand. Here there are roads left untravelled, if we care to consider them. Theories which only now can be put to the test."

"And afterwards?"

"The idea is that you will become a major asset to this nation, concerning yourself with matters of cyber warfare, as it is now understood. Fending off attacks against the government, along with those major institutions on which it relies. This may see you adopting a defensive stance in certain cases, or else delivering attacks to make our enemies stop and think carefully. Ultimately you are to become a standing deterrent, Mr Wylde. A considerable threat. That, at least, is our hope."

"So I'm in the army now?"

The professor thought it over. "Maybe you could say that. Only with the very real threat of a court martial hanging over you at all times."

"Which is where Graves fits into the picture?"

"Yes."

"What's his story? CIA?"

"I'm not sure that Graves belongs to any one organisation or has any particular rank, although he is currently overseer of what is known as Cyber Command. I know him simply as a very powerful individual who has made this centre of ours a reality. And so, if he menaced you at all, then you should know his threats are for real."

"And this centre has been open for a while?"

"No. A mere four months. There are three other

assets on-site at present. And already another seven have come and gone. Either because they failed to live up to their reputations or else disciplinary issues arose which we could not ignore. All the threats that have been made against you so far are very credible, you must understand. There can be no second chances. Personally, I take no pleasure in these severe rules, unlike a number of my colleagues, but they are absolute nonetheless. Especially in your own case, considering the circumstances of your arrival and the havoc you've caused. There are plenty of high-ranking officials who would be only too happy to see you rot in a cell instead."

"OK. I get you."

"But I expect you have been told this already. That there is little margin for error."

"Once or twice."

The Professor nodded, smiled.

"And if I don't make the grade?" Jacob asked.

"Without knowing the specifics, I can guarantee that they will be far less pleasant than your attendance at PROPS."

"PROPS?"

"Yes. That is the name of the complex where you are to be stationed, as well as the overall project to which you've been assigned. Tomorrow our study begins at 7am, at which time you will be expected to catch up quickly with the rest of the group. This shouldn't present a problem. At least this is my hope." Again Radan opened the window, letting in the warm air. They were winding upwards now, ascending a mountain side, and there was nothing to see but forest flashing by.

Professor Radan took the lighter from his pocket and another cigarette from its pack. By the time he had finished this second smoke, their vehicle was slowing down, within sight of a security perimeter. A further three checks were required in the next five minutes as the Ford Explorer was made to halt and have its details verified. Shortly afterwards, they stopped altogether, having reached their final destination.

"Well, goodnight, Mr Wylde. Until tomorrow." With this, the professor climbed down from the back of the Explorer and shut its door behind him. Jacob, instinctively, stayed put. Half a minute later, the security agent got out of the vehicle also and then opened the back door for Jacob to get out.

Evening had arrived and the sky was coloured wine-red with the last of the sun. From where Jacob was stood, he could see a number of low buildings, most of them looking like army barracks, clustered around that rectangular yard where the Ford Explorer had parked up. "Over here," the agent said and together they moved left and entered one of the neighbouring structures through a thick metal door. A military guard was on night duty just inside the building, sat at a small desk. Faced with the new arrival, he looked over at the agent and gave him permission to continue with a slight nod of the head.

On down the corridor they went until stopping halfway along. Then the agent took out a key card and opened another door, off to their left. He held it open for Jacob to walk through. "Welcome home," the man said, with a smirk. And no sooner had Jacob stepped forwards into the room beyond than the door was sealed tight from behind.

CHAPTER 6

Jacob was woken by an intercom fitted into one corner of the ceiling, something which he hadn't noticed the night before (in fact, he hadn't noticed much, being exhausted on arrival, simply stripping to his underclothes and climbing under the blankets on the single bunk).

"Be advised, you now have ten minutes to get washed and dressed," the voice announced.

Jacob had not slept long enough to put a spring into these first steps of the day. There was an element of jet lag involved, but he was also groggy with the newness of this situation: the trouble he had got himself into which was only set to run and run. He had no way of knowing the time, but suspected it was close to six, given that he was supposed to attend a lecture which started at seven in the morning.

First Jacob went over to the small washbasin and cleaned his teeth with the brush and paste waiting for him there. At the same time, he looked around the room. It was Spartan, bright, impersonal, perfectly suited to the situation. Somewhere between a prison cell and a university dorm. There was a self-contained shower unit next to the washbasin and Jacob stepped out of his boxer shorts, tried unsuccessfully to turn the water warm, then stood beneath the cold spray, huffing and puffing. Within the minute, he'd climbed back out, drying himself off with a large white towel.

A single set of drawers lay next to the bed. Jacob opened them up and found blue jeans, white t-shirts, clean underwear, and white socks inside. No sooner had he dressed in a set of these fresh clothes than he heard the sound of his door being unlocked from the corridor, followed by a loud knock. Jacob went over, opened the door, and found a metal tray on the floor at his feet. It looked like a second class breakfast on a commercial airline flight. He carried it back inside and over to the small table. Then he sat down and wasted no time in devouring the food. The meal also included black coffee in a large mug. Thick and strong. Exactly what he needed.

There was another knock at the door, not long afterwards, as Jacob was still munching on a bruised banana. Then the door opened to reveal a young military policeman stood there outside. "OK, Wylde, let's go. Now."

They took the same route as the evening before, only this time in reverse, and then proceeded to cross the entire width of the exercise yard, heading towards the large building across the way. On all sides pine trees created a backdrop to the camp, rising above the military complex to form an imposing barrier. And from the trees, plenty of birdsong could be heard. Meanwhile, up above, the sun had started to climb the cloudless blue sky.

As they neared it, Jacob saw that their destination was a newer building than those other structures on-site. One which appeared to take up at least a square mile. Here the military policeman took out a security pass from his pocket and held this against a control pad fitted into the wall. The door before them then opened with a click.

Once inside, they passed along a corridor whose dark wood finish was buffed to an incredible shine. The walls were painted grey and up by the white-tiled ceiling there were security cameras stationed at close intervals. Jacob's escort led him twenty metres along to a set of double doors on their right-hand side, and then stopped there, waiting for Jacob to open these of his own accord.

The room beyond looked like a lecture hall. There were single desks fanned out, leading downwards to a long wide stage at the bottom. There, before a huge digital screen covering the whole of the back wall, Professor Radan was stood, watching Jacob's entrance. The screen itself was already crowded with all kinds of mathematical figures.

"Good Morning. Mr Wylde."

"Morning."

"Will you please take that desk on which a laptop has been placed for your use and open up 'PROPS 101'."

Jacob looked around, spotted the desk in question, made his way over to it. At the same he counted only three other persons in attendance, already in their chairs, spaced about the room. He sat down, opened the laptop up, and clicked on that icon referred to by the Professor. He could sense that the computer was over-clocked, a serious piece of machinery, and yet, when he peered along its sleek edges, Jacob noticed that were no ports whatsoever to connect it up with any other hardware.

The person sat nearest to Jacob, two table to his left, looked like a surfer or a skateboarder. He was in his late twenties, with blonde unruly hair above a deeply tanned face; a wiry, angular body. While looking over in this direction, Jacob caught his neighbour's eye and nodded at him. In response, the young man gave him a wink.

"Are we online here?" Jacob asked, as quietly as he could.

"Not in any useful way. It's a closed network, strictly for training purposes, and with no license to roam. Plus every single keystroke is faithfully transmitted to the all-seeing eye. Basically we're monitored up the ass."

"Enough, Mr White," said Professor Radan, raising his voice, although it still remained calm. "You have afforded Mr Wylde a warm welcome and so now we return to our studies and pick up from yesterday, if that is OK?"

The young man nodded, "OK Professor, you got it." Then he sat up ramrod straight and stretched his neck theatrically, getting rid of the cricks in it.

"Good, today we shall continue with yesterday's reflections on the cyber attack launched against Estonia in 2007, examining the hallmarks of those Russian military programmers who initiated this conflict." The Professor made a sweeping gesture with his right arm and suddenly the screen became brighter, more clearly defined, bristling with the data residing there. It was touch-sensitive, the vast digital display, and Radan took advantage of this to start pulling down graphic after graphic with swift motions of the hand: dragging statistics across the board, making connections between distant points, disappearing elements and then underscoring new ones. There was no learning curve to speak of. Jacob had been thrown in at the deep end.

This same dizzying storm of facts and figures also appeared on the screen of Jacob's laptop inside an interactive design module. Jacob studied the toolbar on it, working out how to make annotations, examine any of these links in greater detail, or else bring up further summaries. With so much going on, he felt as if his attention was being divided to breaking point. Every time he began to follow one strand of the Professor's thought, Radan seemed to leave off with it and start up with some unrelated theme. And so Jacob found himself trying to hang on in there and take something, anything, away from this lesson, if only to console himself that he was not an absolute dunce.

There was little time to take in his surroundings under these circumstances, but Jacob stole a few brief looks at the two other students. One was a oriental guy in his mid-twenties, wearing brown glasses, a buttoned up white shirt. While directly in front of Jacob, several rows down, was sat a young woman with short black hair, dressed in a blue t-shirt and jeans. Because she had her back to him, it was impossible to tell any more.

Twenty minutes into the class, the bespectacled Asian guy began asking the Professor a series of questions, seeking greater clarification on a matter of software protocol, then persisting with this line of enquiry for another ten minutes. Jacob sensed that this display of curiosity was partly for his own benefit, to serve notice of his classmate's expertise. At his own school, back in the day, it occurred to Jacob that this same kind of behaviour would have amounted to a death wish: putting your hand up and placing your knowledge on open display like that. His own adolescence had been a masterclass of concealment and Jacob's intelligence was nowhere in evidence during school time. It was only during the after-hours computer club that it had ever made itself known.

As the long lecture entered its final hour, Jacob at last began to feel equal to it. At this point, the Professor brought up the Russian hackers' code on the screen, in the form of their captured logbooks, and Jacob studied the programming avidly. It was written in a language he understood as well as anybody else in that room.

At the end of the class, after drawing it to a close,

Professor Radan looked up at Jacob. "A quick word, Mr Wylde, before you head off."

Jacob stayed where he was and waited for the Professor as the older man climbed the steps and then stopped by his desk. "So how did you find that?" Radan asked.

"A bit tricky to begin with," Jacob answered.

"Yes. Well you still have a couple of weeks to adapt."

"Before what?"

"Before I'm obliged to file my initial assessment of you."

"Right."

"Now we have an early lunch. 45 minutes. And afterwards, we resume our studies."

"OK."

The Professor nodded, walked away, and when Jacob turned to watch him go, he saw that the surfer dude was loitering by the doors, aiming a smile in his direction. He stayed put until Jacob had reached him there, and then held out his hand. "The name's Chuck White. Let's do lunch, you and me."

CHAPTER 7

The canteen was two doors down from the lecture room: a modest sized hall, dotted with tables which each had seating for five persons, although for the most part these were hardly occupied. A handful of military personnel sat eating alone or in very small groups; also a few people in civilian dress with the look of scientists, technicians, engineers. The overall atmosphere was subdued and little conversation could be heard inside.

Jacob followed Chuck's lead, picked up a tray, and moved along the food line. There were a couple of hot dishes to choose from. He asked for the fried chicken and it was ladled out for him by a tall middle-aged woman in a blue smock, along with a generous helping of fries. Then he opened up that small refrigerator stocked with soft drinks and took out a Coke can.

"So what else happens here?" Jacob asked.

"Nothing much," Chuck answered. "We're the main event. This place has no purpose other than to facilitate our little group, as far as I can tell. No wonder we're so popular."

They made for an empty table up against one wall and sat down. Chuck picked up his hamburger, took a great bite of it, and spoke with his mouth full. "So what brings you here, Jacob?"

"I dipped into Lockheed Martin's servers last week and outed one of their military prototypes."

Chuck laughed wildly, his cheeks bulging with meat. "I guess that must have caused a big stink in the outside world."

"Front page news."

Chuck looked him over again, as if assessing him in earnest. "Is that right?"

"Yep. And yourself?"

"Me. Well I'm a man with a thousand aliases, but you might know me as Bungalow Bill?"

"No way!"

"I appreciate that response. Good to know that my reputation still goes before me in certain circles."

"Well I'm a long-time admirer of your work."

"And there was me expecting you to be a two-bit punk who got lucky one time only."

"Maybe I did."

"Don't give me that fake modesty bull, Wylde. No-one pulls off a stunt like the one you described without Jedi Class mind powers."

"So why exactly are you here now?"

"A little stunt of my own I unleashed four months back. Turned every computer inside my local FBI branch into an old school arcade machine. Pac-Man, Missile Command, Defender, all the old-time greats. Basically I refashioned their "secure" network as a backwards looking games console."

Jacob laughed loudly, shredded chicken shooting from his mouth.

"Yeh. Seemed like a good idea at the time. Although now I have my doubts…" Chuck looked around him as if to justify these same suspicions.

"You any idea where in the states we are?" Jacob asked.

"Who's to say we're even on US soil? I mean it does look like the homeland, I'll grant you that, but there's no knowing for sure. Maybe it's a huge mock-up of the

Rockies and we're really on a Saudi airbase, out in the desert somewhere."

"And that lecture this morning, that's what we do all day?"

"For the most part, although you've got surprise exams to look forward to as well. These get sprung on us without warning and we've had two so far. Hardcore simulations of real-time events. That's where we lost three of our original number who weren't up to speed."

"And what's the story with those laptops? I couldn't work out the specs on them, but they seem like pretty advanced machines."

"They're fast, but you've seen nothing of the real hardware yet. That stuff is kept out of our way until the time of the big tests. Then we get led into a room that's decked out with some crazy ass technology. Which is maybe not surprising when you consider what we're meant to do with it eventually."

"Which is what?"

"Bring countries to their knees. Stop others from doing the same to us."

"And I take it there's no chance of opting out?"

"I suggest you tread very carefully, bro. Because the alternatives are not good. Same goes for slacking off. Best to look lively, hit the books, keep your grades up."

"Spoken like a true maverick."

Chuck shrugged. "Hey, listen you want to go the bad boy route, that's fine by me. Only you have been warned."

"So who's in charge here, ultimately."

"On-site? That would be the camp Kommandant. A ball-breaker by the name of Colonel Havers."

"He's a tough cookie then?"

"The man is a hater. Better watch your step, bucko. There's nothing he likes more than coming down on one of our number like a big old heap of bricks"

"And Professor Radan?"

"His back-story is off-limits, but the man's Iranian and you can only figure that he was pulled out of that country, one way or another, and then set to work here. I get the feeling he's the classic burnt-out type: a former genius put out to pasture with nothing left for him to do but hand down his knowledge. He's a sorrowful individual, I'll tell you that much. That said, the man is worth listening to. He clearly knows his bits from his bytes. Taught me a thing or two which is no mean feat."

"Even if you do say so yourself."

"Exactly."

"And what about the classmates?"

Chuck aimed his fork in the direction of their Oriental colleague, sat alone at a table in the dead centre of the floor. "Well, first up we have Zhao Min, and basically he hates your guts already, without needing to speak to you first, simply because of what you represent – more competition. You're looking at the kind of shorty who's only interest in life is being classed as number one in everything he does."

"Then I can see how we might be having problems, me and him," Jacob said.

"O-ho! Check you out! The great white hope! Personally, I blame it on the kid's upbringing. All that tiger baby nonsense. Being made to learn basic algebra before he could wipe his own butt. Zhao's the only one in here who signed up for this gig and didn't have his ass hauled in for crimes against the state."

"He volunteered to come here?"

"The freak insisted on it. Even knowing what conditions were like and the lack of freedoms involved. Still he quit an advanced program at MIT and signed off on three years of his life. Wanted to study with the Professor, whatever the cost. Believes Radan is the only man on the planet who can still teach him anything."

"And her?" Jacob nodded at the young woman. She was staring down at her food and poking it around the plate.

"That's Rebecca Kent. Went by the name of plainjane. Part of the Outage Collective, operating out of Toronto for a time. Into political activism. Tangling with multinationals. Oil companies and the like. A sick talent, but as for you hitting on her, Jacob – and I'm one step ahead of you here – forget about it. Let's just say that she doesn't do social interaction. I've had maybe fifty words out of Comrade Kent in the last three months. Not that I've blessed her with the full Chuck White charm, you understand."

"Who said anything about hitting on her?"

"Listen, it's bad enough for me, being stuck in here without female companionship, but at your time of life...What are you, 20? 21?"

"19."

" Dang! Your hormones must be screaming blue murder right now – all them little sperm-men running riot with nowhere special to go."

"Not exactly how I'd put it."

Chuck slurped up the last of his coke, a sly smile on his face. "Oh, that's right. I got you figured now. You're the romantic type. Jacob Wylde's looking for love!"

CHAPTER 8

Jacob Wylde's first month at PROPS passed quickly, aided by the strict routine which he had no choice but to observe. After the long lecture in the morning, and the long lecture in the afternoon, dinner was served in the canteen, much the same as lunch. Then the three attendees were returned to their rooms, although their working day was still not at an end. For while none of Professor Radan's students were entrusted with their laptops outside of classroom hours – except for Zhao Min – they were still handed a great variety of printed matter to study, analyse, and correct of an evening. Or else they were asked to write summaries of those figures and formulas and scenarios they had touched upon that day. What's more, all these assignments were expected to be handed in the following morning for Professor Radan to assess.

All of this intense study not only helped to pass the time, Jacob also threw himself into it to avoid considering anything else. To fight off worries about his mother and what was happening back at home. In this way, the here and now functioned as a refuge for him, despite the heavy workload.

Usually, by the time 10pm rolled around, Jacob would be absolutely shattered, running on empty, having digested a wealth of new information. Then he would crash on his bunk and fall asleep quickly, although most nights his dreams provided him with little release. Instead, rather than leaving off from the day's calculations, his unconscious brain used them as a springboard, and there appeared in his mind's eye a manic string of numbers and letters, all of them woven together like a giant spider's thread, stretching out endlessly into the far reaches of space, forever pulsing with energy.

It was a strange and powerful experience which went on for hours into the night. What's more, it seemed to Jacob that this fantastical vision was becoming more and more vivid each time, and taking on a life of its own...

When morning arrived, Jacob would wake to a dull throbbing headache, centred between his eyes, although the first coffee of the day started to lifted this curse, and an hour later, the pain would be largely gone.

The first couple of study papers that Jacob handed to Radan were dismissed quickly, but not cruelly, by the Professor. One on the future of quantum computing. Another on the AES algorithm.

"I want more coherence, Mr Wylde. Greater fluency. This was very disappointing. I require an improvement from you. And soon."

It was not that Jacob was slow, only that he'd had far less schooling than any of the others. And so, for the first time in his life, he found himself wishing he had gone to Cambridge University on that scholarship offered to him earlier, if only because it would have made his life that much easier now. It frustrated Jacob that while he understood these workings in principle, he struggled to describe them on paper – lacking the terminology to explain what he knew already and break it down into clear steps. Almost the opposite was true of Zhao Min. For Jacob's classmate was always weaving elaborate sentences full of theory and calculus. And although Zhao's interest in these topics was no doubt real, he was also sending a message to the others, Jacob sensed. Trying to bully his rivals with all this jargon he'd picked up over the years.

Although these demonstrations of Zhao's unsettled Jacob at first, soon he came to see them as a positive thing and they definitely spurred him on. In the figure of Zhao Min he had exactly what he needed: an irritating rival who Jacob wanted to take down. By week three, encouraged by this rivalry, Jacob started to speak up for himself in class, as a way of laying down his own markers and thinking out loud. His written papers also began showing signs of improvement and merited encouraging words, if not outright praise from the Professor.

In the afternoon their lessons took a more practical turn and it was here Jacob truly came into his own. Now the order of the day was executing tasks, accessing data-sets, improvising stratagems, all the time confronted by ever more elaborate cryptography. As Professor Radan set them these tests, he encouraged the group to consider time as a vital factor in their completion. The clock, he informed them, was always ticking. Wit this in mind, Jacob could not help but notice that he was always either first or second in the class to take his hands away from the keyboard and stop typing in frantic commands. And this he found greatly encouraging.

In contrast to his feelings towards Zhao Min, Jacob's friendship with Chuck White only grew. He considered it an honour to fraternise with the legend that was Bungalow Bill (in many people's opinion, including his own, one of the greatest hackers of the last decade. A trailblazer who, for the sheer hell of it, had been putting the big boys' noses out of joint since the late nineties). The two of them sat together every mealtime in the canteen and let off steam, kidded around, shot the breeze. Exactly the kind of release which Jacob needed.

The other major distraction was Rebecca Kent. And the crush on her Jacob was starting to develop. Every opportunity he had, he took to staring at Rebecca from afar. He still knew next to nothing about this young woman and could think of no way to discover more. During their classes together, Rebecca's own verbal contributions were non-existent and Professor Radan seemed to make an allowance for her quietness which he did not extend to his other pupils. Under these circumstances, there was nothing for it but to stare at the back of her neck. In the canteen, meanwhile, Jacob viewed Rebecca in profile as she sat there at her regular table, staring down at her food, at one with her mysterious thoughts. Dwelling on her past, Jacob imagined. A past he knew nothing about. And yet despite this lack of knowledge, Jacob's attraction to her only continued to grow, and he spent as much time as he could considering what to do about it – trying to think of a way he might overcome her solitude and get to know her better.

At the end of Jacob's fourth week at PROPS, during lunch, Chuck caught him looking Rebecca's way yet again.

"I told you Jacob, you've got no chance."

"What?"

"No chance whatsoever. She's a living, breathing firewall. Trust me. This is one romance which is never going to blossom, my man."

"I get the feeling she must have blown you out already, Chuck, seeing as how you won't shut up about her."

"What? Me? Try wooing Little Miss Autistic? No way. That's a fool's game."

"Yeh, I believe you."

"I'm more concerned with this next simulation they're set to spring on us. Five weeks now and nothing since the last big exam. It can only be a matter of time and I'd just as soon we got it out of the way."

"You'll be fine," Jacob said.

"Hell, I know that," Chuck answered. "I was thinking about your sorry ass."

CHAPTER 9

It was during the fifth week, on a Thursday evening, that the next simulation occurred. Completely out of the blue. Jacob was sat at the table in his room, feeling drowsy, having just written a short paper on Feistel networks, and was already thinking about hitting the sack. Then he heard a knock outside and almost immediately the door opened up. It was his regular military escort, Purvis, standing there.

"We have a situation, Wylde. A major incident. I'm to escort you to the Operations Room now."

"They would have to do this at the end of the day," Jacob muttered.

"Quit bitching. I want you out of this room in twenty seconds."

Together they left the barracks and crossed the parade ground in the late summer heat, a wild red sunset overhead. Entering the main PROPS complex, they passed the canteen, the lecture room, and then kept on going until they'd reached the far end of the deserted corridor, outside of Jacob's regular boundaries. Here Purvis pulled what looked like a wafer-thin strip of silicon from his shirt pocket and proceeded to insert this into an unmarked groove contained in the wall. There was a delay of ten seconds and then the reinforced metal door relented through a series of clicks.

On entering this secure area, the corridor became dimmer than before, with small ghostly LED bulbs fitted into the ceiling above. The two men passed a number of heavy-set doors, the spaces beyond them completely closed off, and then Purvis slowed to a halt in front of another entrance on their right, with a guard stood outside of it. This second man turned now and placed his own security card into the encryption panel. Then he pulled the door open directly for Jacob to walk through.

The area inside was large, dome-shaped, with a sunken floor and a huge digital screen on the far wall, twelve feet high, and spanning one third of the room's circumference. This gently curving screen was divided into different data sets, awash with 3D computer modelling in a state of tremendous flux. Either side of the screen, the gently curving walls stretched away, housing a series of tall cabinets. Each of these cabinets had a smoky perspex front beyond which could be seen evidence of serious hardware. Most striking of all was the cumulative hum from these same machines. It was a low and constant sound, suggestive of immense processing power.

In the centre of the room lay a wide semi-circular table at which Zhao, Chuck, and Rebecca were already seated, a large monitor in front of each, along with a keyboard and mouse. Professor Radan was on his feet behind them, pacing about. It was exactly as Chuck had described the room to Jacob earlier, and yet he was still bowled over by these first impressions as he stepped down onto the floor proper, moved over to the table, and lowered himself into the one available chair. Then he looked about the room again, returning to those cabinets arrayed around its walls, knowing that they amounted to a single supercomputer which was now at his own disposal. As Jacob surveyed these units, counting their number, he was interrupted by Radan who put one hand on the back of his chair. "Enough, Mr Wylde. You are not here to drool over this technology, but to put it to good use. We have an ongoing incident here which requires your immediate attention."

"OK."

Jacob switched on the monitor and was greeted by the usual PROPS interface from class, although here there were a number of new icons he had not seen before.

"There is no time for an elaborate briefing," Radan continued. "We cannot sit you down and walk you through this. You must imagine that a major disaster is occurring in the here and now. To be more specific, a trojan virus has been activated in a Nuclear facility over in New Jersey at the behest of a hostile foreign power. This action occurred approximately three hours earlier and has now resulted in progressive damage to two of the four main centrifuges. On top of this, all attempts to re-access the principle control system have so far failed. If this situation continues unchecked, we will be faced with nuclear meltdown. Your objectives then are to access the facility, stem this attack, and re-assume overall control before disaster strikes. Tonight I want to learn what impact, if any, you can have on a situation like this in the course of two hours. If you will all please open up the Princeling icon. Everything that you need, in theory, is there."

No sooner had Radan mentioned the time-limit for this simulation than it showed up in the top right corner of their screens, counting downwards, adding to the pressure. Jacob glimpsed it once and then brought up the schematics of the nuclear facility. He rotated this 3-D modelling from every possible angle while considering his overall approach, realising that this exercise would call upon many of those subjects they had studied intensely during the last five weeks.

His first step was to try accessing the operating system using standard protocol as described in the plant manual. Then, finding his way barred repeatedly, Jacob tried creating his own backdoor. But after gaining access to the system for a matter of seconds, his permission was revoked and he was kicked back out again. Seven times in a row, Jacob's efforts were similarly repelled, but on the eight occasion, and with a careful tweak of the software, he managed to mask his entrance so that it looked like an extension of the virus itself. This allowed him to gain full admittance to the operating control system. With forty-eight minutes gone, Jacob had found his way in.

He looked up and around for a brief moment at everybody else. Chuck, Rebecca, Zhao. In each case their faces were creased with frowns, lost to their strenuous mental efforts. As for Jacob himself, he was now using five windows at one time: running diagnostics tools, seeking to retain his invisibility, while still searching out the ultimate culprit concealed within the system – the one which was spewing out false directives and issuing destructive commands. At the same time, the PROP's supercomputer accommodated this multitasking effortlessly. The key for Jacob was to concentrate all of that processing power amassed in the room and bring his own precision to bear.

It was at the ninety-minute mark that Jacob finally located the malign rootkit which had hijacked the PLC software, hiding in the Statement List. At once he set about countering it with code of his own devising: ingenious, purposeful, and deadly. He was in the zone, his focus absolute, at one with this objective. Typing furiously as the seconds flew by.

With less than three minutes left, Jacob finally succeeded in seizing upon the malware and expelling it for good. And yet he was only distantly aware of having completed the task – unable to switch off that intense concentration which had seen him triumph. Instead his mind pushed on, continued to accelerate, sending him plunging headlong into an altered mental state. Suddenly Jacob was confronted with his recurring vision again, the one which haunted his dreams, only it was now more vivid than ever: a chain of numbers in perpetual motion spiralling away into space. He could feel the draw of all that pulsating energy, and the longer Jacob looked upon these hurtling threads of code, the greater the temptation to get closer to them still, as close as was possible, until he had fused with these structures and got to know them from the inside-out. This struck him as both an alluring and terrifying possibility. But on this occasion, it was Jacob's fear which finally won out, and with it the great determination to pull away…

When he regained consciousness, Jacob was now sat on the floor, propped against the table. Professor Radan was stood leaning over him, a hand on his shoulder, trying to bring him around. "Jacob…Jacob?"

He climbed up off the ground and got back into his chair, more embarrassed than anything, wanting to make light of his situation. "I'm fine. I wasn't out for long, was I?"

"Maybe thirty seconds."

"Just a bit tired."

"And you're sure that's all that was?" Radan looked at Jacob closely.

"I'm positive. I just nodded off. It's been a long day."

Still the Professor considered his student, troubled by what he'd just seen. "Ok, Mr Wylde. You'll be glad to hear that you're all to have an extra hour in bed tomorrow morning as a special dispensation. I suggest you, for one, make full use of it." With this, Radan stood up straight and moved away towards one of cabinets. "Now you may all leave…"

The sentry outside the Operations Room led all four of them back out of the building. As they crossed the parade ground in the humid dark, a large half-moon high above them, Chuck put an arm round Jacob's shoulder. "You alright, champ?"

"Must admit, I thought Radan was going to pack me off to the medical bay, although I'm plenty glad he didn't."

"I reckon that would have made life difficult for the Professor as well."

"How do you mean?"

"Well, Colonel Havers is only looking for an excuse to kick us all into touch, and a fainting disease would certainly raise questions about your own fitness for duty. Basically, I don't think Radan wants to lose his most valuable player."

At this, Zhao Min snorted.

"Sorry Zhao. I forgot you're the only here who's worth Radan's attention."

"Your words, White. Not mine."

"Right, so I take it you completed the task?" Chuck added.

"That question is of no concern to you."

Suddenly, it was Rebecca who spoke up, addressing Jacob directly. "That ever happened to you before?" She asked.

"No. Never."

She nodded. "You suffer from sleep disorders?"

"Kind of." Jacob scolded himself for this honesty.

She nodded again.

"Why?"

Rebecca shrugged. "Only I knew someone once who experienced the same kind of complaint."

"And what happened to him?" Jacob asked.

"I couldn't tell you."

"That's comforting."

Rebecca smiled.

CHAPTER 10

Rebecca Kent was sat in the front row of the lecture room, straining
to retain her focus. Today it was a real struggle to follow Radan's lecture on cryptanalysis in the final years of World War Two (at that moment, he'd made another leap forward and was considering the late mathematical papers of Alan Turing, along with how they might be adopted for the present day). Rebecca was not alone in being greatly distracted that morning. All of the group were waiting to discover how they'd fared the night before and what their fates would be as a result.

For her part, Rebecca had managed to access the operating control system of the nuclear plant after one hour. Then she'd started to run a series of integrity checks, scanning the system in depth, but in the process she'd let her guard down for a whole minute and thus alerted the virus to her presence. As a result she'd been shut back out of the system with forty minutes to go. And for all her frantic efforts, there was not enough time to correct the mistake.

Rebecca had to hope that she'd still done enough to scrape through, but it was not impossible that this current lecture would prove to be her last. That she'd be taken from her room this evening, bundled into a car, and driven god knows where. Just like those others who'd formed part of the original intake of talent at PROPS, three months earlier.

It was not that she was altogether happy with the current arrangement, but wherever else they sent her, it would certainly not be as lax as here. Yes, there were strict procedures inside the complex, but it was a new set-up all the same, largely untested, and therefore not without one or two flaws. What she needed was the time to highlight enough of these to make escape a real possibility. In her own low-key way, Rebecca had been scouting this physical environment since day one, subjecting every last inch of the complex to her scrutiny, on the lookout for weaknesses, oversights, structural lapses. There was no way she could reconcile herself to remaining at PROPS, working for a government which she didn't believe in and thought guilty of great global harm. In fact it was an indignity for her to be trained for their own dark purposes; an indignity which none of the others felt. For Chuck White, hacking was all about the money. For Zhao Min, it was about the glory. And Jacob Wylde? Well, he did it simply because he could, and because this fact never failed to surprise him – the scope of his own freakish abilities.

Enough about Wylde already, Rebecca told herself. But now that his name had popped into her mind, she could sense his eyes on her again, several seats back. In the canteen they were even more blatant, these romantic inspections, and he'd developed a habit of staring at her repeatedly while she ate. As if he thought she was holding something of herself back. Something of great value which he wanted to discover for himself. Rebecca, for her own part, was not all of one mind when it came to thinking about this strange boy. But increasingly these thoughts seemed to take up more of her spare time and she scolded herself for this and tried changing the topic in her head. Wylde was cute, but so what? There were much more pressing concerns to deal with.

Now Radan drew the lecture to a close and looked up at his students, acknowledging their expectancy. "I want you to know that every one of you performed adequately last night. There is room for improvement, of course, but still I must declare myself relatively pleased with you all."

"Praise be," said Chuck.

"Now I would like to discuss the finer points of your individual approaches on a one-to-one basis. Mr White, if you would be so good as to postpone your lunch for one hour, we can conduct this briefing now."

"Okey-dokey. You're the boss."

In the canteen, Jacob was aware of a new social dynamic, with Chuck absent from the room. He carried his food to the usual table and sat down, but failed to settle. Maybe the moment had arrived for him to take the bold step he'd long imagined? Jacob asked this question of himself several times, trying to work up the necessary courage. Then, with his heart in his mouth, he rose from the seat and transported his tray over to where Rebecca was dining. She turned to look at him when he was half-way there and tracked his progress coolly. Jacob stopped before her.

"What's up – you lost your best buddy?" She asked.

"Just thought I'd join you, if you don't mind."

There was no shrug. No nothing. And Jacob had to decide for himself if she minded or not. After a few seconds more, he sat down opposite and still Rebecca did not take her eye off of him. It was as if she was paying Jacob back for all his stolen glances with this one almighty stare.

"So what is it you'd like to talk about?" she asked.

"I guess I'm just curious about you," he said.

"I see."

"Wondered where exactly you come from, for one thing."

"A small town in Missouri. You wouldn't know it from Adam."

"This place have a name by chance?"

"Yep."

Jacob waited in vain for Rebecca to elaborate, then tried another leading question. "How old are you then?"

"Twenty."

"And you're in here for some kind of political protest?"

"Who told you that – Bungalow Bill?" She used Chuck's tag with scorn.

"Is it true?"

Rebecca picked up her club sandwich, considered her answer carefully. "Well, let's just say I'm not in it for the kicks like you two crazy cats."

"What's your problem with Chuck?"

"I think he's full of it, your friend."

"Come on, the man's a legend."

"Who told you that? Chuck?"

"You must know about his reputation. You've got to give him his due."

"That was all a long time ago. Tell me, what's he done of late? Last I heard he was blackmailing large firms. Threatening them with DNS poisoning. Not exactly the stuff of legend."

"Well Radan must have thought highly of him to have brought him here. And let's be honest, Chuck wouldn't have lasted this long if he wasn't equipped to handle it."

"Maybe. We'll see." She picked up the small carton and took a sip of her orange juice, then put it back down. Again she looked at Jacob closely all the while. "You completed that simulation last night, didn't you?"

Jacob nodded.

"That puts you in a very special category, you know."

"You don't know that Chuck didn't complete it as well. You don't know for sure that Zhao didn't manage to either."

"I know all right," she said. "You're out there on your own. Only problem is it doesn't appear to be agreeing with your health."

"So who was this other person you were talking about. The one who experienced something similar?"

"Just an old friend." As if anxious to bring their conversation to a close, Rebecca looked at the clock on the wall and rose up from her chair. "Well, Jacob. It's been real nice talking to you."

CHAPTER 11

For once, Professor Radan was absent as they trailed into the lecture room at 7am the next morning. Jacob, Chuck, Rebecca, and Zhao all took their seats and each of them tried booting up their laptops, but without supervision there was no starting these machines. So they sat there instead and awaited Radan's arrival.

As the wall clock showed ten minutes past the hour, Zhao Min turned anxiously in his chair, not for the first time, and looked towards the entrance.

"What's up, Zhao?" queried Chuck. "Your teacher gone left you? Don't panic, son. Just go with the flow."

"Don't be so infantile, White," Zhao snapped back.

"Fun loving, Zhao. Not infantile – fun loving. Something you wouldn't know anything about. Comes with having had a regular childhood, unlike yourself. Bet your mother was working that performance related number on you from day one. Probably didn't get any breast milk until you'd done your homework for the day. Maybe that explains why you never rose much above five feet tall."

"At least I had parents to guide me, White. I believe you were raised by a television set while your mother was out flipping burgers to pay the rent."

"Oh. Like. Wow. Is that how it's going to be? Are we to disrespect each other's kinfolk until there's a clear winner here? One tip for you though: I don't think you're gonna make too many friends by flaunting your stable home life. The rest of us are from the other end of town." He gestured vaguely to Jacob and Rebecca. "And let's not forget why you're here, grasshopper. At least we're all hand-picked cyber-baddies. As far as I can tell, you're only in attendance to improve your grade average."

At this, Zhao's eyes flashed and he reared up out of his chair. In response Chuck stood up also and began shadow boxing. Dancing on the spot. "Come on, short stuff! Let's go. Put up them dukes!"

Zhao clenched both fists and considered a further escalation. Then Rebecca spoke softly from her chair, claiming everybody's attention. "I can see you now, White, back in the school yard: selling out your fellow nerds to get with the cool crowd. The kind of kid who always wanted it both ways."

"Jeez. Did you not hear what he said, Comrade Kent, about dysfunctional families? I was sticking up for the dead-end kids. The angels with dirty faces."

"Looked more like plain bullying to me."

Chuck turned to look at Jacob. "I guess there's no need to ask what you think, Jacob. That would be exactly the same as our resident anarchist here." Jacob said nothing while Chuck shook his head, mock disconsolate. Then, with this scene played out, Professor Radan suddenly burst through the doors looking flustered. A rarity for him.

"I've just got off the phone with Graves. We have a real-world situation happening right now and he wants you all on it as a matter of priority. You've been given temporary authorisation to go live." As Radan remained by the door, catching his breath, he held it open for all four of them to follow.

Once outside, the Professor led the way to the far end of the corridor, inserted his security pass, and opened up the section door. Nearing the Operations Room, he shouted to the guard on duty, "Get it open. Now!"

CHAPTER 12

On entering the Operations Room, the four of them moved swiftly to the semi-circular table and claimed the same seats as last time. Jacob looked up at the huge digital display. It contained a single large map of the United State, slashed with linear markings, dotted with flashing ruby-red points.

"So what are we faced with, Professor?" Zhao Min asked.

"An incursion against the US power grid. No way of knowing what exactly this group is up to, but they've compromised the system entirely and we have no idea what they've got planned next."

"And the source of this intrusion?" Zhao continued.

"It appears to be coming from Russia. We have no more specific information than that, and so it's impossible to tell whether this is officially sanctioned or the work of a crime syndicate. The important thing right now is to stem it."

"You wouldn't be messing with us here would you, Professor?" Chuck asked.

"Please be assured, Mr White, this is no elaborate training exercise. What you are seeing here are real-world systems coming under heavy attack. I would have liked to postpone this moment for another couple of months, but we are seriously out-manned at present and every available programmer is being assigned to this emergency. Therefore your urgent assistance is required."

"So what's expected of us here?" Rebecca asked.

"It's been decided by Cyber Command that you will try and open up a second front: locate the exact source of this trouble and then give these people a taste of their own medicine while our regular programmers seek to put out the fire. Nobody's expecting miracles here – just do what you can."

On each of the group's monitors there were several new icons on display, representing a dizzying array of software, and it was clear that they were fully connected to the outside world. But as each of them did as Radan requested, and began to seek out these intruders, they were immediately confronted with a huge obstacle. The enemy had seen fit to encrypt their own network with an incredibly powerful algorithm and their digital footprints couldn't be pursued beyond it.

"That's an AES cipher. The one we studied two weeks ago," commented Zhao Min.

"It's brutal, that's what it is," Chuck said. Then he turned and looked at Jacob. "You see any way past this perfect storm?"

"Maybe," he answered, scrolling down the screen.

"Well if you can get us in then I can certainly dish out the punishment. Reckon Rebecca can too, if she doesn't mind colluding against communist powers."

"Nonsense, Wylde," blurted out Zhao. "It can't be hacked. Not a 128-bit Rijndael algorithm. Certainly not in a matter of hours."

Jacob shrugged, already gearing up for the challenge. "Only one way to find out," he answered.

It was all about finding a single thread to unravel, staring at the seemingly random combinations until a sense of harmony emerged. With this in mind, Jacob began sifting through a huge stream of binary data, looking for a jolt of recognition. The hint of an underlying design. And the longer he looked, the more immersed Jacob became in this intense task.

It was twenty minutes in when a sequence of thirty-two digits suddenly leaped out at him. Like a line of text written with the caps lock on. The numbers made stunning sense to Jacob's mind. Now he began to explore this glaring fragment and relate it back to those written characters all around. His fingers thundered against the keys in precise sequence and again he felt that rush of blood to the head, coursing through his brain. A supreme mental agility. The rest of the room was now reduced to awestruck spectators. It was clear just how profound Jacob's concentration had become and none of them dared break it. Twenty-eight minutes later the encryption fell to his efforts and the hackers' true location stood revealed. The group now had everything it needed and their enemy was in plain view.

"That's it! We're in!" Chuck shouted. "Time to rain down a fire storm on their heads. Here's a little something I call 'A Bungalow Bill Smackdown'!" He cracked his knuckles and started in on the keyboard. Meanwhile, it was clear from Rebecca's intense concentration that she was one step ahead of him, already launching her own attack. Zhao too began making his contribution, although there was no disguising the look on his face. It was one of defeat.

Now Professor Radan stepped away from his vantage point against one wall, where he had been standing immobile for the best part of an hour, taking in everything. He came forward to the desk and placed a hand on Jacob's shoulder. "Everything all right, Mr Wylde?"

It sounded to Jacob's mind like a wake-up call from a

long way off and he struggled to respond to it, nodding his head slowly.

"Good. That's your work done for today. I would ask that you take a back seat now and allow your colleagues to take over."

"Yeh. OK." Jacob felt dazed, drained, distant.

During the next hour, Rebecca, Chuck, and Zhao stepped up to the plate and sowed enormous havoc, taking the battle all the way back to its source, revealed now as the heart of downtown St Petersburg. On the main digital display at the front of the room, the map had been extended to include Russia in its scope and reveal the true lines of battle. The assembled enemy force was clearly huge, issuing from a hundred separate terminals, but now that these positions stood unveiled, they were sitting ducks for a devastating counter-offensive.

"There. On the screen. Look," Rebecca said, after they'd been hard at it for another half-hour. She could see that the flashpoints were disappearing one by one in quick succession like the candles on a cake.

"Hallelujah!" said Chuck. "We've got those bastards on the run. Them Russkis just caught themselves an awful case of Cyber VD. Whole network is dripping with puss right now."

"Not exactly how I would have put it, Mr White. However, I believe you're assessment is fundamentally sound," remarked Radan.

Chuck wheeled his chair over to where Jacob was sat and slapped him on the back. "The force is immense in this kid. I've seen some whirlwinds in my time, but that was plain freaky. Whatever it was you tapped into there was not of this planet."

"You must understand that what you've just experienced was only a skirmish," said Radan.

"Not what you were saying before," suggested Chuck.

"A notable skirmish then, Mr White, but I don't want you thinking that together you've saved the western world single-handedly."

"Maybe not, but we did a pretty good job of protecting one of its major institutions."

"You did OK. Let's call it a qualified success."

At that point a man entered the Operations Room dressed in full, flawless uniform; a great many signs of distinction attached to his green jacket breast. He was clearly a soldier of impressive rank. Tall, broad, muscled, in his late fifties. There were spiky tufts of grey hair on top of his head, not unlike a grizzled bird of prey. It was the first Jacob had seen of Colonel Havers in the flesh. He knew the Camp Commander only by reputation. But that reputation chimed with the figure who was standing before them now, hands on his hips, looking over at Professor Radan.

"And?" He said, his voice low and gravelly.

"They acquitted themselves admirably," the Professor answered.

Havers brushed this assessment away. "Well that's what they're here for as I understand it."

Radan looked back at him, added nothing more.

Havers now turned his attention to those seated at the table. "Considering the crimes most of you have committed, this is the least you might be expected to do. Doesn't even cover the interest on your felonies as far as I'm concerned. You've all got a long long way to go in paying this country back." He continued staring at them for some time, and then his eyes came to rest on Jacob in particular, or at least that's how it felt to him, unless this was only his mind playing tricks. "I'd be obliged to you, Professor Radan, if you completed a report on this incident and had that on my desk by 14.00 hours tomorrow," Havers continued.

"Of course."

"Good." Havers looked away from Jacob and ran his eyes over the group as a whole. "You all have a nice day," he said in parting, flashing a malicious smile before he turned and left.

"There's gratitude," Chuck said, once the Colonel was out of the room.

"It doesn't detract from your achievements here," Radan said. "And believe me, that is not going to pass unnoticed."

CHAPTER 13

Afterwards, they lunched in the canteen. Jacob was still feeling weak as they entered and so Chuck steered him over to their usual table. "Here you go, champ. Sit yourself down here. I'll go get the food. Take it you're sticking with the fried chicken?"

"Yeh, and can you grab me a black coffee as well."

"Strong as hell?"

Jacob nodded.

"Consider it done."

Jacob looked over at Rebecca as she queued for her own meal. In truth, he would have liked to have sat down next to her again and continue with their talk from last time, but felt unable to make a good impression in his sorry state.

When Chuck returned, Jacob ate less than half of the food on his plate, but felt much better for the large hit of caffeine.

"Listen," Chuck said, "one day we're going to get an overnight pass for all our good work here. It has to happen. Maybe not this month, or the month after that, but they can't keep us locked down forever. Especially now that we've started to prove our worth."

"Why not?" Jacob asked.

Chuck swatted away this pessimism with one hand. "And when we do, I'm taking you to Paradiso. The best lap-dancing bar known to man. Back in the good old days when I was clearing fifty grand a day through my illegal activities...Man, you should have seen it. I was treated like pervert royalty."

Jacob chuckled, shook his head. Then they both watched as Zhao Min got up from his table and walked over to the toilets. He still looked pale and haggard from before. In answer to their own curiosity, he stared back at the pair, picked out Jacob, threw him a hateful look.

"You've got him mighty pissed, Jacob," Chuck said. "Of course his whole idea was to show you up as a one-hit wonder, nowhere near his league."

"Doesn't look like that's going to happen."

"Nope. Looks to me like you've handed him his ass." Chuck dabbed his lips with a paper napkin. "I'd watch your back though, as a precaution. I reckon he's an unforgiving little bastard. And remember what I said about those other students who failed to make the grade. Nothing I can prove – but I have him down as a snitch as well. Don't think he's above knocking on Havers's door, trying to make trouble for the competition."

"I think I'm going to have a word. Try and straighten this out now."

"You're wasting your time."

Jacob shrugged. "I still want to say my piece." And so he rose from his seat and followed Zhao into the bathroom. There was no sign of him at the urinals, but Jacob could hear a retching sound from one of the cubicles. Someone puking up their guts.

When Zhao came out of the stall, he was holding a bunch of toilet roll to his mouth. He stopped, surprised, and stared back at Jacob. "What do you want?"

"I wanted to try and draw a line under this ill-feeling. Can't see how it's going to do either of us any favours in the long run."

Zhao threw the soiled tissue in the bin and began running the warm tap. He looked at Jacob through the mirror. "I don't think the long run is something you need to concern yourself with, Wylde."

"Meaning what?"

"You're on the verge of a major burn-out. It's plain to see. I don't expect that you'll be here with us much longer. That's the thing with you freaks of nature: at some point, you tend to blow up."

Jacob shook his head. "You want to keep this rivalry up? Fine. Let's see where it gets you."

Zhao dried his hands with a paper towel, allowed himself a thin smile. "The truth is I don't have to do anything, Wylde, except bide my time and wait for you to implode."

CHAPTER 14

When Jacob returned to his room that evening, there was a portable CD player on his bedside table, and a stack of discs beside it. No doubt it was Professor Radan who had made these items appear suddenly as a reward for their morning's work. It was certainly not Colonel Havers's doing.

Jacob sat down on his bed, sifted through the discs, and found that every one of them met with his approval. They included Ascent by Wiley, Vibezz by Theophilus London, and Matangi by MIA. Placing the first of these into the machine, he pressed play, lay back against the bunk, and listened to track one. It was only with his head resting against the pillow that Jacob realised each of these albums had featured on his iPod back home. This was surely no coincidence. In all likelihood, the security services must have gone back to the house, under Wilkins's direction, and turned over Jacob's room for every last trace of available evidence. He imagined this intrusion now, saw his mother put through hell again, and it was all Jacob could do to stop from crying.

He had to hope that Chuck was right and that their effectiveness would see more concessions come their way. Today it was a CD player. Maybe a long distance phone call would be permitted in time? Surely it was not impossible. This was the very least that his mother deserved.

Jacob's father had left the family home when Jacob himself was six years of age. It had happened without any warning as far as the young boy was concerned. The sky had suddenly caved in on their life together and things had never been the same again. Shortly afterwards – after the divorce had come through – his father had left the country, emigrated to Australia, and started a new life there. As if he'd written off both Jacob and his mother as a bad mistake, best forgotten about. Now he had a new wife and two daughters – step-sisters who Jacob had never met. Nor had Jacob set eyes on his father in all these years since the day he'd up and left them.

It had been hard for his mother to cope with this absence, Jacob knew. The emotional wound had not been quick to heal, and yet she'd always fought to rise above it: working two jobs to keep a roof over their heads, food on the table, and to encourage Jacob's growing interest in computing by buying him the first of several machines. All of this his mother had achieved in spite of the dark clouds that gathered on her own horizon from time to time and got the better of her. Days in a row when it was all she could do to get up and go through the motions. What Jacob's mother described as her "seasonal blues".

In truth, this was part of the reason he'd never gone to Cambridge University, although Jacob had never admitted as much to his mother. His ongoing concern for her well-being. Not that she'd welcomed his concern. In fact his mother was angry at him for not leaving:

"These kinds of chances come along once. You want to spend the rest of your life round here when the world is yours for the asking?"

"I'll just put it off for the year..."

"You say that now..."

And she was right. The next year came and went and Jacob only stayed put. Not that he hadn't made any progress in this intervening time. In fact, there was good reason to believe that he was on the verge of making it big through his apps business. On top of this, he'd also been head-hunted by a new computer games start-up called Trex, based in Liverpool at the Baltic Triangle. He'd gone and had talks with these people and discussed the possibility of going to work for them for a decent salary, as well as shares in the fledgling company. But the problem was the ease with which he could perform the work they'd asked of him. That was what had caused Jacob to mess up everything: the need to test himself further. It was this impulse which had led him to The DoubleDareCrew, and to steal away with Project Eames, and to give up his freedom in the process. With these thoughts churning around inside his brain, Jacob felt for the off button on his CD Player, and turned over on his side. It took him twenty minutes to fall asleep, and when he did, there was to be no rest.

CHAPTER 15

When Jacob was woken next morning by the intercom, he discovered that the sheets beneath him were drenched in sweat, sticking to his body. He struggled to get up out of bed and drag himself under the shower, desperate for that knock on the door and his first coffee of the day.

It had been another costly night of dreams – his sleeping brain once again prey to mathematical visions of feverish intensity. A ceaseless storm of fast moving numbers which had kept on at him throughout the night. Stepping out of the cold shower, Jacob remained far from refreshed. He put a hand to his forehead to feel the heat it was still giving off.

The day improved, half an hour later, when Radan began their lecture with word of a new development. The screen behind him was empty for once and his topic was other than calculus.

"Last night I had the opportunity to speak with Mr Graves, in his capacity as head of Cyber Command, and argue that your effectiveness will be severely hindered if you stay inside this fixed bubble. I told him it is vital now that you are able to keep abreast of contemporary developments in all relevant fields. If they want to see the best work from you, it makes little tactical sense to keep your wings clipped."

"Amen to that," said Chuck.

"I am happy to report that Mr Graves consented in part to my proposals, and as a result you are are to be permitted a greater degree of freedom on a trial basis. To begin with, you are free to take the laptops with you after class and use them as you will. Of course, they will still be subject to intense scrutiny, however you are to be allowed limited online access within carefully monitored parameters."

"How limited are we talking about?" Rebecca asked.

"Well, there is to be no email facility available to you, no instant messaging, or any other means of communication, but you will be able to browse a large array of chosen educational databases, university libraries, and daily newspapers. Of course, your keystrokes will continue to be logged in real-time and needless to say your web history will be carefully catalogued as well. Also, random spot-checks will remain in force."

"And what about erotic content, Professor?" Chuck asked.

"No, Mr White. Erotic content must remain out of bounds also."

"No fair."

"Furthermore," Radan went on, "it has been decided that you may leave your rooms and socialise with each other of an evening within the confines of the main barracks. After dinner and until the hour of ten pm."

"What's Havers make of all this?" Chuck asked with a grin.

In answer, Radan allowed himself a thin smile, suppressing a much wider one. "The important question is what does Mr Graves think. And the answer is that he can see the wisdom in my arguments. I have taught you as much as I can within these boundaries. We need now to extend them. You are, without doubt, the most promising class it has ever been my privilege to work with and I see no reason why you shouldn't continue to go from strength to strength."

Chuck sighed. "I guess that leaves me and you free to play chess together of an evening, Zhao. I'm looking forward to laughing about our former misunderstandings and becoming the best of friends."

Zhao Min turned round to look at him. "Needless to say, you would only be wasting your time. I will never answer the door to you, White."

"Finally," said Radan, "please be assured that if this greater trust proves justified then I will do what I can to have further privileges extended to you. I know what it is like to remain under suspicion at all times, and how counter-productive this can be..."

After the morning lecture, it was Jacob's turn to have a one-on-one session with the Professor in order to review his performance in the Operations Room. They sat alone in the lecture hall at two neighbouring desks and Radan began by studying his student's face in detail. "How are you feeling today, Mr Wylde?"

"Right as rain."

"So you slept normally last night?"

"Like a log."

"And yet you look terrible."

"Thanks."

Radan looked uneasy, conflicted. "I think you understand that I have a balancing act to perform here. If I refer you to the medical staff then it will arouse the interest of Colonel Havers. A man who is not sympathetic to our project, nor to any of its personnel."

"I'll be fine, Professor, but thanks."

"I do hope so." Radan answered.

"And what about my assessment?"

Radan held up his hands. "There is nothing more to

be said about that. Your work was uniformly excellent. My only concern is for your fragile state of health."

CHAPTER 16

The dark green walls of Colonel Havers's office were festooned with framed certificates, professional awards, and pictures of Havers stood next to other men who were more powerful than he was. As for the Colonel himself, he was leaning over his desk as noon struck, staring down at the latest order from Cyber Command. Again he stared at this paper accusingly, shook his head from side to side. "Absolute horseshit," he said.

The button on his phone flashed twice and made a trilling sound. Havers put it on speaker. "What is it?"

"It's Charles Graves, Colonel. He's got back in touch and made himself available for a brief video link-up. Suggests you contact him now."

"OK. I'm switching the monitor on. Put me through."

The large screen on his desk came to life and within seconds a crystal-clear image of Graves dominated its centre. He appeared to be on a plane, judging by the little background Havers could see, and his impassive stare was already trained on the Colonel himself. Those pale blue eyes losing nothing of their power to disturb, even at distance. "Good Afternoon, Colonel Havers. What can I do for you?"

"Good Afternoon, sir. It's about this latest order I've received."

"Is there some some confusion about it?"

"Well the first I knew of this was when it arrived on my desk this morning."

"And you have a problem with this mandate?"

"With all due respect, I have several."

"Such as."

"Well the whole idea of giving these young people any more than freedom than what they've already got strikes me as wrong-headed."

"Your scepticism is duly noted, Colonel. But you're not suggesting that you're better qualified to make this decision than I am?"

"No sir. But I think it's worth noting that Professor Radan has a soft spot for every single one of these detainees. That is as clear as day and I believe it's clouding his judgement."

"And yet you cannot fault the results. Their performance yesterday was a triumph, whatever way you care to look at it."

"I'm only saying that there's a balance to be struck."

"OK, and of course I value your input, Colonel. However, for the time being, we're going to allow this to proceed."

"And am I too issue them with condoms as well?"

Graves paused for a few seconds, and then leant closer to the camera. "Spare me the sarcasm, Havers. I know this post at PROPS is not the one you were looking for, but we still expect you to be professional."

"My professionalism, Mr Graves, has never been called into question."

"Nor am I calling it into question today, Colonel. I am simply asking for your full co-operation here."

"Yes sir. If you think this is the best way forward."

"I do. Professor Radan made a very convincing case. Also, this will give us a better understanding of how the group ticks. Think of it as a behavioural study. If we allow their interpersonal relationships to develop then this will provide us with useful data. Data which we might then exploit."

For the first time, Havers brightened slightly in conceding this fact. "Yes sir. That is also true. But I still believe Radan should have notified me first."

"The Professor answers to me directly, Colonel. You know that."

"Yes, sir. But as a matter of courtesy, if nothing else, he might have informed me in advance."

Graves looked down and away, as if scanning a document. "May we consider this matter concluded for now?"

"Yes sir. Of course."

"Good.

*

Half an hour later, there was a knock at Havers's door. He stayed sat behind his desk and waited a good twenty seconds until a second knock was heard. "Come in," he said eventually.

Professor Radan entered the office, walked slowly over to the Colonel's table and stood by the opposing chair.

"I guess you'd better sit down," Havers said, after another pause.

"What can I do for you, Colonel?" Radan asked.

"Whatever idea you may have formed in your mind up till now, I thought it important to remind you that this complex is not an Ivy League campus but a secure military facility. Highly secure. And you need to understand that the freedoms here are strictly limited for good reason."

"I understand that a careful balance needs to be struck," Radan answered.

"Where you see a balance, I might see a dangerous surrender of authority."

"That is true. I expect our viewpoints are world's apart."

"But make no mistake, any trespass, of any type, and I will see to it personally that these young anarchists are sent somewhere a whole lot more suitable. I will also make darn sure that you are personally held to account for their crimes."

Radan said nothing.

"So we understand each other?"

The Professor stared back, deadly serious as well."Yes. I'm certain that we do."

"This is not the end of it, Radan. Rest assured of that."

CHAPTER 17

After their new freedoms had been announced, Rebecca waited two days and then called on Jacob Wylde in the evening, committing herself to this action without knowing exactly why. Her motives were confused and refused to keep still.

Of course, there was her desire to escape PROPS to consider, and how this might be served by the young man in Room 7A. The temptation to bring Jacob Wylde's immense skills into the frame and use them for her own ends. Certainly with these special talents at her disposal there was every chance he could provide Rebecca with a small window of opportunity, especially now that that their access to the laptops had increased. But at the same time, Rebecca was not without feelings for Jacob as well, intrigued by this curious gift of his which kept weighing down his soul. Both a blessing and a curse. Also she thought she recognised in him a loyal, generous, over-active heart, capable of much more than the usual kindnesses. And physically, she found herself attracted to the young Englishman as well, wanting to act on what her senses kept telling her.

After knocking twice, Rebecca heard footsteps inside his room and then Jacob opened up the door. The look on his face one of startled disbelief.

"Just thought I'd drop by," she said.

"OK. I mean good. Come in."

He stepped away from the door and Rebecca walked straight over to his small table and pulled up a chair. Meanwhile Jacob moved over to the small refrigerator, newly installed. "I've got pineapple juice or Gatorade?"

"I'll take the Gatorade, thanks."

He pulled the bottle out and carried it to the table, then sat down on the spare chair. His mind still racing, she could tell.

"How did you find that exercise today?" Jacob asked.

"A lot like the exercise yesterday," Rebecca answered.

"Yeh. I know what you mean."

Jacob continued with his nervous small talk for the next fifteen minutes and Rebecca helped it along, obliging him with straight answers, looking for a way to move the conversation on. "Wonder when they're going to call on our services again?" Jacob asked. "I mean for real."

"Soon, I hope. The more use we are to them, the better our chances of gaining extra privileges," she said.

"Yep." He looked sombre all of a sudden, as if she'd triggered a specific thought.

"Have you got family on the other side, Jacob?"

"My mother, yes. That's about it. What about yourself?"

She shook her head, smiled. "Nope."

"That must be tough."

"Tend to think of it as a blessing myself. Nobody need worry themselves stupid."

"Maybe you've got a point," he admitted.

"So your mother's on her own now?"

"She is. Yes."

"Sorry."

"The thing is she gets really low sometimes and I've always been there to help raise her spirits, stop her falling into a rut." Jacob was spacing his words out, pausing to hold himself together.

"That's got to be hard."

He nodded. "Yeah. But at least I've got someone waiting and hoping to see me again. I mean I know you said it's good to have nobody, and I can see what you're saying, but all the same…"

"Well this is not a new situation for me and I dealt with it a long time ago. I mean I never had that growing up – an adult I could count on – and so this…" She gestured to the dorm room, "is nothing I can't handle."

"I'm not saying I can't handle it either…" Jacob sounded defensive, having shown a degree of weakness.

"No, I know. But it's only natural that you would miss your home."

"Well, I'm not ruling out the possibility of my seeing it again." Now Jacob sounded defiant.

"I'd say that's a tall order."

"Maybe," his eyes flashed. "But isn't that what we're meant to specialise in? Isn't that why they've got us both here: to pull rabbits out of hats?"

Rebecca smiled. Jacob looked down at his hands, briefly preoccupied. Then he stared up at her with that maddening look, like she was totally precious to him already. "Listen, anything I can ever do to help you, Rebecca, I will. Whatever it is."

She paused for a time, then replied to him. "That's a hell of a big promise, Jacob. Considering how little we know one another."

"I know."

"OK then. I'll bear that in mind."

Rebecca got up as if to leave, and Jacob got up also. They were stood one foot away. Rebecca looked at Jacob intently, then she stepped forwards and moved in close until her lips were on top of his own. Her tongue entered Jacob's mouth and he met it readily and the kiss lasted a full minute before the two of them pulled away. Jacob then ran his top lip over the bottom one, as if trying to interpret what had just happened. "You're awful sure of yourself," he said.

"You're right. I had this strange feeling you weren't going to take offence."

Jacob laughed. "You know I've been waiting for that to happen since the first day I saw you."

"There you go," she said, heading for the door. "Dreams can come true."

It was certainly the start of something between them and during the next month this thing began to grow. They spent more time together which Jacob always craved, anxious to buy more minutes with Rebecca alone. He found that he couldn't decide what he wanted more. The chance to explore her body or to tell her everything about himself. Where he came from and what he hoped to become. Once Jacob got started, there was no stopping this talk. It was as if he'd been waiting all his life to let down his guard.

Rebecca, for her part, didn't open up much, even though she encouraged it in Jacob. In this, she had the habits of a lifetime to overcome. That vital, guarded secrecy. One of those survival techniques which had served her well from the age of fifteen and made a life on the streets possible. This same instinct which made her wary of her own heart and the direction it was starting to take.

To the best of their knowledge, there were no surveillance devices planted in their rooms, but all the same they dove under the covers when the time came, almost instinctively, as if they still couldn't rule the possibility out. For this same reason, Jacob turned the music up loud on his CD player to drown out their intimacies and stop them from reaching other ears.

Under the sheets, during these wordless moments, Jacob watched Rebecca's eyes blazing in the semi-darkness. It was here she responded fully to the passion in him and met it head-on.

One persistent, troubling thought occurred to Rebecca during this time. The possibility that they were glad to see this flourish – the powers that be – and that in falling for Jacob Wylde she would only be aiding their plans. Wasn't it actually in their interest to see such a relationship develop? The two of them becoming ever more reliant on each other? This meant that certain threats could be made. And for this reason a part of her wanted to put a stop to this altogether and tell Jacob they needed to cool things off completely. Every morning, in the cold early light, she felt this way. But then her resolution lost ground throughout the day, and by the time evening rolled around, Rebecca was ready and willing to meet Jacob alone and happy for them to spend this time together.

And yet it was far from resolved in her mind, this situation. Whether she was embarking on a full-blown romance or only getting ready to exploit him when the time came. Rebecca's thoughts and feelings continued to fluctuate wildly. Then there was the impulsive promise Jacob had made to her earlier, which featured in her mind like a get-out-of-jail card, ready for immediate use.

'Anything I can ever do to help you, Rebecca, I will. Whatever it is.'

She considered these words often and gave some thought as to how this promise might best be deployed. Was Jacob Wylde her asset, her lover, or both? It was still not clear to Rebecca Kent.

CHAPTER 18

It was two months exactly since Jacob had first arrived at PROPS when they came for him in the middle of the night. The door was flung wide open and three soldiers entered the room, causing him to snap awake and sit up straight in bed. First he thought they were going to inform him his presence was required in the Operations Room. Either for another simulation – even more inconvenient than the last time – or else an actual emergency for the group to put down. But then the trio pushed forward and branched out, one of them shining a powerful torch beam in his direction. Jacob raised one hand instinctively to shield his eyes from the glare while trying to look through his fingers. In this way he saw that at least one automatic weapon was trained on his body. The men stopped two yards short of the bunk and started barking directives for him to follow.

"Out of bed now and get on the floor. Face down."

"Do it now. You will not be told again."

"All right. Hold on."

Jacob climbed down from his bed and got on his knees. As he began lowering himself flat against the stone floor, the weight of a boot was applied between his shoulder blades and he found himself spread-eagled.

"What the…..!?"

Both arms were wrenched behind his back. Then Jacob felt plastic binding up against his wrists, pulled tighter, then tighter again, until there was no slack whatsoever.

"Get him up." Two of the soldiers grabbed an armpit each and hauled Jacob to his feet.

"You're not gonna tell me what this is about?" Jacob's question was only met with silence. Two of the soldiers moved to either side of him and locked arms with his own. The third had put his weapon down and begun turning the room over already, wrenching drawers from their cabinet. Jacob realised, without a shadow of a doubt, that this situation was deadly serious. Some wild accusation had been levelled against him which he could not possibly know.

He was led from the main barracks and across the parade ground in the dead still of the night. A couple of times Jacob stumbled on account of the soldiers' relentless pace, and they caught him again, kept him upright, continued hurrying their prisoner along.

Next he was brought to that small, square, anonymous building to the left of the main complex. The one Jacob had wondered about before. Its main entrance was pushed open and he was forced down a short dim corridor with exposed concrete walls, then brought to a halt outside an olive-green metal door, a series of large keyholes studded into its surface. One of the soldiers pushed this door open and Jacob was shoved inside the room beyond it. A stark holding facility, featureless except for a thin wooden shelf and a lavatory in one corner. Without another word, the door was slammed shut and the light from the corridor was instantly snuffed out. He heard the sound of several keys turning in their locks. Neither of his captors had bothered to remove the cuffs from his wrists.

Stepping forwards carefully, Jacob moved himself over to the wooden surface and sat down there in the darkness, trying to still the mental confusion and allow for some clarity of thought. For all the world, he couldn't make sense of this sudden assault.

Who had it in for him? The obvious candidates were Colonel Havers, Zhao Min, or else a combination of the two. But surely there would come a moment for him to launch a proper defence and set the record straight? Jacob also had to hope that when Radan learnt of this wrongful accusation, he would step forward, spring into action, and put a stop to this nightmare. Round and round these thought went, but there was no way to profit by them until he discovered what was truly going on. Reluctantly then, Jacob lifted his legs up and onto the hard surface and tried getting a little sleep in spite of everything.

In the event, he grabbed less than an hour.

It was Colonel Havers himself who entered the cell just before dawn. A stark light bulb was switched on by one of the two guards who also stepped inside the room and this sudden bright light meant that the Colonel's jubilation was plain to see. He walked up to where Jacob was laying on his side, and as Jacob tried manoeuvring himself around to get his feet on the floor, Havers watched this effort up close.

"Whatever information you've been given, I'm telling you now it's absolutely wrong. I haven't done a thing. This need straightening out," Jacob said.

"But I have straightened things out, Wylde. Absolutely. And that is why you're here."

"What is it I'm meant to have done?"

"You're wasting your time, playing the innocent. The mistake you made was in thinking you could run rings around everyone. Happily I had some say in who ran the forensic spot check on your laptop this time around. The man I put on this case happens to be top of his field within the CIA. As a personal favour, he paid us a visit last week and ran the latest test on your little group in place of Pavese, Radan's old pal. And what does O'Hara find, after hours and hours of rooting through your hardware, but that your recorded keystrokes are no more than an elaborate bluff. Then he digs and he digs and he digs, and in that way he discovers what's really been going on. Not hours of homework for the good professor. No. Seems you've spent the last few weeks liaising with your Chinese paymasters instead."

"You're making this up as you go along!" Jacob protested.

Havers shook his head vigorously. "No, Wylde. Spare me the outrage. This has been verified and then verified again. Your guilty as hell."

"This is a set up, Havers. I'm telling you. I've done nothing whatsoever!"

At this the old soldier lunged forward, grabbed hold of Jacob by the throat, and squeezed with his right hand. "You'll address me as Colonel, Wylde! Who the hell do you think you are?"

Jacob stared back hatefully, struggling to breathe, the colour rising in his face. There was a slight movement from one of the guards, off in the background – as if to bring Havers to his senses – and at this, the Colonel let go, shoving Jacob back against the wall. "You sicken me to the stomach, you little prick."

"I want to speak to Radan."

"No way. I'm sending you off on a voyage of discovery without any tearful goodbyes."

"What are you talking about?"

"You're going to a place where you don't get to come back. This move is final."

"Where are you sending me?"

Havers grinned. "Somewhere real private." And with this, he turned his back on the prisoner and strode out of the room.

After the Colonel had exited the cell, one of the guards had Jacob stand up. He turned him around and let him out of his cuffs. Then he departed also. Jacob brought a hand up to his throat. He could still feel the pressure from Havers's grip, burning his windpipe. Either the bastard was central to this conspiracy or else his malice had blinded him to what was really going on. Jacob wasn't sure which theory was worse.

Several hours passed by and then Jacob heard a faint droning sound outside. Minutes later, the same guard as before entered and placed him back in handcuffs. He led Jacob beyond the holding cell and outside the building. Jacob saw now that it was a Chinook helicopter which had made the earlier noise. The copter was hovering above the centre of the parade ground, mere inches off the floor. Its rotor blades still turning, ready for immediate take-off. As the guard escorted him towards the craft, Jacob twisted his neck a hundred degrees and tried looking over at the long window of the canteen. Several figures were stood there behind the glass, watching the action unfold, but Jacob swiftly picked her out of the small crowd. Rebecca had brought a hand up to her face and pressed it against her mouth. Her eyes were strictly horrified. Jacob moved his lips and mouthed the words he'd been meaning to say. Then the guard redirected his stare and Jacob was made to face forwards. Away from the young woman he loved.

CHAPTER 19

Professor Radan knocked on the door to Colonel Havers's office. When there was no answer, he looked again to the man's secretary, stationed at a small desk outside. "You told me he's in there," Radan said.

"He is. And if you'll just wait a few moments, I'm sure he'll see you. Why not try knocking again?"

But Radan had had enough of waiting already and so he opened the door up for himself and walked straight through. Havers was sat behind his desk, rocking gently against the thick padding of a black leather chair. But at the sight of the Professor, he lurched forward in his seat, hands splayed against the tabletop. "What the hell do you think you're doing Radan! Entering this office without clear permission?"

"Spare my your sanctimony, Havers. What have you done with Wylde?"

"The foreign agent you're referring to is currently on his way to an appropriate holding facility." The colonel's face beamed with this knowledge.

"Foreign agent! That's total nonsense.'"

"Far from it."

"And how did you arrive at this deduction?"

"You know who I had look at their laptops last week?"

"That task had been assigned to Pavese."

"Yes, and then I had it reassigned to Thomas O'Hara

instead. As for Pavese, well I think your friend has got a few questions to answer. This took place right under his nose. Chances are he'll be hauled off before a closed committee on the subject."

"And how exactly did O'Hara come by this incriminating evidence?"

"It was there on the computer, hidden under several hundred layers of bullshit. The recent correspondence with Chinese intelligence. Wylde was leaving the back door open for them here at PROPS so they could enter at their leisure and take a good look around. In return, they'd arranged to wire money into a Swiss bank account, and the first large payment had already been made. No doubt that was only the beginning of this arrangement. I reckon they had big plans for Wylde in the coming months."

Radan took out his cigarettes. "Or at least that is the impression O'Hara was left with," he answered.

"And you ain't smoking those things in here, either," Havers said.

The Professor tapped the end of a cigarette against the box. "I think that you are making a grave mistake."

"Oh yeh?"

"Yes I do. If you're claiming that Wylde was engaged in espionage work."

"I'm not saying that. O'Hara is. A senior analyst at the Central Intelligence Agency. His preliminary report is already on your desk. I suggest you go and read it before storming in here, shooting off your mouth. Try studying the facts first."

"So Graves knows about this?"

"Of course Graves knows. Who do you think I went to with this in the first place. He turned it over to his top people and they only confirmed what O'Hara had discovered. This has been double and triple checked. Wylde is guilty of this crime. Consorting with the

Chinese. And as for his famed genius, my own hunch is that it was purely a hoax. He was somehow being helped out by their people. But I'm sure this will all come out in the wash. The important thing is that we've brought him to book."

"So you thought nothing of going over my head?"

Again Havers laughed. "I think you're getting a little confused about the command structure around here. Anyway, you're the one who likes to miss his colleagues out of the decision making process. Isn't that how you got these ridiculous freedoms approved to begin with. The ones that led to this god-awful mess ."

"I still should have been consulted."

"So you could come to Wylde's defence and drag this out on some technicality?"

"You think that verifying whether or not a crime has been committed, and who the perpetrator really is, is not worthy of due consideration?"

"And you think you could have done a better job of discovering the truth than a team of senior analysts at the Pentagon?"

"Perhaps, yes."

"Maybe. Once upon a time. But from what I understand it, your own powers have ebbed to nothing. Which is why you're here, working as a supply teacher for a bunch of disturbed freaks."

"I think I need to speak with Graves."

"You can try. My guess is Mr Graves will be looking to distance himself from your good self for the time being. Reckon that hotline of yours is liable to become a whole lot less reliable from now on. This happened on your watch, Radan, and so your own involvement in the whole affair is something I think we'll need to consider as well."

"So you are now saying that I am part of some overall plot?"

"I'm saying that I'm not prepared to rule that out at this time. I'll be launching my own investigation this end, and then we'll see what we see. In the meantime, any more irregularities occur and I'll make sure that you're suspended from you post immediately. Don't forget, we saved your sorry ass to begin with by getting you out of Iran."

"That's not exactly how I remember it."

"No?"

The Professor shook his head.

"Well I wouldn't expect anything other than ingratitude from a man such as yourself. But make no mistake, your days here at PROPS are strictly numbered if I have any say in it." With this, the Colonel stood up and pointed sternly at the door. "That's us done for today."

Chapter 20

When Jacob failed to arrive for their morning lecture, Rebecca knew that this could only mean trouble, one way or another. Her first thought was that he'd been taken sick, no longer able to deal with the mental strain placed on him at PROPS. The price he paid for his astonishing brilliance must have been exacted from Jacob in one terrible payment, triggering some kind of breakdown which had landed him in the sickbay.

As Radan began his lecture, nothing was said on the subject of his star pupil's disappearance, but the Professor's troubled expression, and even the way he delivered the lecture – detached, remote, otherwise absorbed – did not bode well. Rebecca wanted to ask him what was going on, but at the same time felt reluctant to display her concerns, because she didn't want their closeness on record, and also on account of not wishing to have her worst fears confirmed. It was Chuck White who put it to Radan plainly, half an hour in.

"Where's Jacob, Professor?"

"I don't know, Mr White. I shall be talking with Colonel Havers after this lecture is over to find out what is going on." The professor's own ignorance – real or imaginary – did not set Rebecca's mind at ease either.

At lunch, she sat down at her usual table and made

a start on her chilli. Then there was a loud commotion outside, attracting interest from the whole dining hall. Everybody stopped eating and watched as the Chinook descended from the sky. It was a singular event. Never had Rebecca seen such a landing in all her time at PROPS. It made her consider the possibility that Jacob was being transferred from here to a better equipped medical facility. With this thought in mind she got up, moved away from her regular table and positioned herself over by the window, best placed to see what happened next. As she stared out at the parade ground, Chuck came and sat opposite her, unannounced.

"What do you reckon?" He said.

She shrugged. "Your guess is as good as mine."

"Maybe he's ill?"

"It's a possibility." She said no more, unwilling to share her own distress.

It was ten minutes later that Jacob was led out of the small building to their left and towards the helicopter, cuffed from behind, treated like a prisoner and not a patient. Clearly he'd been charged with something serious. As Rebecca rose from the table and looked on, Jacob twisted round and caught sight of her standing there. He opened his mouth and made his declaration and Rebecca read those words Jacob had long had in mind. Then the guard pushed him forwards, towards the waiting craft. No sooner had the two men climbed on board than the helicopter began its vertical rise. Wherever they were headed, it could only mean a world of trouble for Jacob Wylde.

"Holy shit," said Chuck. "Looks like Jacob is screwed."

"You know nothing about this?"

"Nothing at all."

"You didn't have him mixed up in some stupid scheme?"

"I should be asking the same thing of you, Rebecca. You're the one he spends all his spare time with."

She stared at White. Hesitated. "I think we need to go and see Havers together."

He arched his eyebrows, held up his hands. "I hear what you're saying. Only I don't see the benefit in us both getting canned as well."

"So I'll have to do this alone?"

"Listen, unless I'm mistaken, you won't have to go to the trouble of beating down Havers's door. I suspect he'll be pretty damn insistent on speaking to all of us before the day is through."

In the afternoon, Zhao Min, Chuck, and Rebecca returned to the hall for their second lecture of the day. As Chuck had suggested, they did not need to wait long for a summons to arrive. A guard entered the room, five minutes in, and said that Chuck White's presence was required at once. He got up from the desk, appearing highly sober, especially by his own goofy standards, and made his way over to the exit. It was another forty-five minutes before Chuck returned, looking no less serious than when he'd left.

Next the guard asked Zhao Min to follow him as well. Zhao's expression was a whole lot different to Chuck's. He looked like he didn't have a care in the world. As if it would be a pleasure to volunteer everything that he knew and hammer the nails in Jacob's coffin. It was an hour and ten minutes before Zhao returned also. Then the guard called Rebecca up from her seat as well and led her directly to Colonel Havers's office.

"Sit down, Kent," was the first thing he said.

She did as asked. Took the chair in front of the Colonel's wide imposing desk.

"You know why you're here?"

"I saw Wylde being led away earlier."

"And put two and two together. Good. Because that's exactly what I want to talk about. Jacob Wylde."

"It's not a subject that I know all that much about."

Havers smiled, tauntingly. "No?"

Rebecca shook her head, told herself to keep cool.

"Now there may be nothing linking you to Wylde's actions as far as we can tell, but there's no doubting the two of you were close."

"Not particularly."

"You're sure about that?"

"I'm positive, yes."

"Then you won't mind us turning your room over or requisitioning your laptop again."

She shrugged. "Do what you've got to do..."

"You know, I think you look a little sad today, Rebecca. Almost teary-eyed. What is it? The wrong time of the month?"

He was trying to bait her. "I look no different from usual," she answered coldly.

"And so you're telling me you'll have no difficult in forgetting about Jacob Wylde?"

"I'm a past master at putting people out of my mind."

The Colonel looked about her face as if searching for its key. "I think you're lying, Rebecca. And believe me, given your closeness to Wylde, we'll be picking over every last link between you and him. Also, whatever privileges you've enjoyed up till now are officially a thing of the past. All that spring break bullcrap is gone forever. Best thing you can do is keep your head down and up your workload. You are here to be of service to your country. Something that a great many others do willingly, voluntarily, considering it an honour. Christ knows you don't fall into that precious group."

She stared back at him, said nothing

"You want to go back in your shell and stop speaking,

fine. I don't give a damn, either way. But now you get to look me in the eye and say 'Yes, Colonel. I understand.'"

"Yes, Colonel. I understand."

He smiled at her, showed off his teeth. "You're not going to last are you, Kent? I give you one month before you try pulling off a smart-ass move like some avenging fury. Only a matter of time before you act on all that hatred. Your eyes are drowning in it."

Chapter 21

The flight in the Chinook was brief. It took the pilot less than twenty minutes to reach their destination and touch the helicopter down on a clearly marked landing pad. As seen from the air, it appeared to be part of a large military airbase, complete with several criss-crossing runways and countless outbuildings.

Jacob and his escort were met on arrival by a small Jeep, stationed just beyond the painted circle. The guard led him over to the vehicle and transferred Jacob to the custody of three US marines in combat fatigues. One in the driving seat. The other two in the back.

As soon as Jacob had climbed up, the Jeep took off at speed, racing along the slip road. As it did so, Jacob saw a large sign flash by, set back on a trim lawn: Seymour Johnson Airbase: Home of the 4th Fighter Wing.

After crossing over a couple of runways, they began following the wide tarmac of a third until a huge plane rolled into view. The Jeep kept on straight, making for this transport vessel, and finally stopped a minute later directly beneath its tail. Staring ahead, Jacob studied the large aft ramp of a Boeing C-17 Globemaster III. It was fully extended, ready for its cargo.

The marines got out first and then escorted Jacob up the broad ramp into the massive hold. It was a largely empty structure, with a number of primitive seats attached to the bulkhead. Here a further two marines were already present.

"He's the delivery?" said one of the seated men.

"Yup. This is him."

"All this for one little runt. A two day round trip when I should be on leave right now." The soldier stared at Jacob directly. "Pull any kind of stunt, cowboy, and I'll be only happy to terminate this mission double-quick."

The Globemaster took off twenty minutes later and the four soldiers began their watch, alternating on the hour, all of them sitting opposite Jacob during this time, giving him their full attention. Only the marine who'd complained about his suspended leave broke from this pattern: oiling and sharpening the blade of his large Bowie knife with a whetstone, then looking over at Jacob occasionally as if there was nothing he'd like more than to plunge the weapon inside of his chest. The others kept to the far end of the plane while off-duty: playing cards, talking among themselves, and then falling silent, succumbing to the monotony of the flight.

For Jacob, it was not long before the journey started to drag. Then, at some point, it began to feel endless. Two of the four turbo fan engines on the Boeing lay directly behind the bulkhead where Jacob was sat, and their loud drone and heavy vibrations hampered his attempts to rest. Hours passed. And then more hours again. He dropped off, woke up, dropped off again, slumped against the exposed metal frame. On the very last occasion he snapped awake, Jacob was freezing cold, shivering fiercely. The soldier opposite addressed him at this point. "You gonna be a good boy and put on your winter clothing without any dumb ass stunts?"

He nodded, dazed. Another marine was called over and untied Jacob briefly, stood back while the prisoner put his arms through the sleeves of a thick green army coat. Then he was cuffed again.

Fifty minutes later, the plane finally came into land. The descent itself was rocky, lifting Jacob from his seat and testing the limits of his safety belt. On touchdown, the plane skidded to the left, struggled to find traction, as if the ground beneath it was treacherous and slick.

When the Globemaster had reached a stop, the aft ramp was slowly lowered again. Jacob was brought to his feet and escorted forwards by those two marines who had first navigated him around the airbase. With the ramp fully extended, all three of them began their descent into the frozen wastes below.

Jacob was dirty, tired, unprepared for this severe climate. Conditions here were blistering cold, even with the jacket given to him earlier. It was no match for those brutal icy winds sweeping across the hostile terrain, animating the heavy snowfall. Moreover, it was an astonishing landscape which confronted him. One which had the impact of a dream, given Jacob's great fatigue. To the right of the landing strip lay a beach of black volcanic sand, with pack ice beyond it, and a large glacier away to the right. And then, strangest of all, in the other direction, a gigantic black structure loomed out of the dazzling whiteness. A hulking man-made design, built into an existing lava shelf, fashioned from many acres of metal and glass. Its construction was smooth, all curved, and put Jacob in mind of a great crouched predator getting ready to pounce.

He was led across the icy runway in the direction of this building and taken to that large set of doors at the foot of the jet-black structure. One of the marines punched in a code. Then he stepped back and allowed the second marine to follow suit. Seconds later the doors were opened from within and their party stepped forward to leave the blizzard behind.

A burly, bearded man was sat there waiting for them in a small entrance area behind a wide steel desk. He wore a navy blue uniform without any markings. One of the marines took a sheaf of papers from the inside of his coat and lay them flat on the table for the guard's careful inspection. Then the bureaucracy of the transfer took place, with both parties signing off on this exchange. Meanwhile the other marine removed Jacob's cuffs, relieved him of his outerwear. As he did so, Jacob looked down at his red-raw wrists for several moments, waiting for his circulation to return.

With the exchange concluded, the marines left the way they'd arrived without another word, glad to be shut of their "delivery", ready for the homewards leg. As they departed, the guard himself stood up and displayed his immense physique. "My name is Garcia," he said. "Your full induction takes place tomorrow. Right now I'm to take you to your cell."

Garcia led the way over to a metal door in the far wall. He pressed the button to one side of it and the door opened onto a waiting elevator. As the two of them entered, Garcia took out a strange looking key which resembled a surgeon's scalpel and turned this anti-clockwise in the panel to his right. The elevator rose for thirty seconds, with hushed efficiency, and then stopped at another level. Here they walked out into a long corridor stretching away in both directions. Garcia took hold of Jacob's elbow and directed him leftwards along the passageway. Its walls were dull, grey, punctuated by a small number of bronze-coloured doors spaced out at wide intervals. Jacob counted four of them in total. After a couple of minutes they stopped before a fifth entrance, equally anonymous, and Garcia showed Jacob inside.

His first impression of the cell was one of perfectly designed confinement. He could see no grounds for optimism. It felt to Jacob as if his fate was now sealed tight.

CHAPTER 22

Next day in class, Professor Radan was even more distracted than the day before. A far cry from his usual self, he stumbled over his lecture notes on the Twofish algorithm, the tiredness in his face all too apparent, as if he'd not slept at all the previous night. Something that Rebecca could sympathise with. For her part she'd lain there on her bunk, staring up at the darkness, her mind turning over for hours at a time. Unable to locate a single positive.

Her feelings for Jacob were genuine, this she now knew. It was more than self-interest. The proof of her attachment was evident in the sharp pain she'd felt when watching him being dragged away; the extent to which Rebecca was haunted by his utterly bleak prospects.

At first, when she'd considered involving Jacob in a break-out, Rebecca had reckoned on a scenario in which they would split up on the road as soon as was practicable and take their chances alone. But then, as time passed, her plans had started to alter. She'd thought less and less about going her own separate way once they'd fled the compound, and instead imagined them on the run together, forging new identities and disappearing from view. Creating a joint life. Rebecca had only been waiting for the right moment to put this escape plan to Jacob Wylde. A moment that was gone forever. Now it all seemed miserable, hopeless.

At lunch, she sat alone in the canteen. Rebecca's mood so obviously grim that Chuck White didn't dare join her, although she could tell he was thinking about it. Then she hauled herself back into the lecture hall to resume taking notes on her laptop on the subject of disruptive technologies.

It was forty-five minutes later that a private message appeared suddenly on Rebecca's computer, centre of screen, impossible to ignore. There was no way it should have been able to evade the rigid filters fitted to the machine, and yet here it was.

She stared at its contents.

At 7pm the door to your room will stand open. Take a right and keep to the middle of the hallway. Take a left at the end of the corridor and do the same again. Fifty metres up on your left there is a door which reads 'Supplies'. Open that door, enter, and close the door behind. Here a suggestion will be put to you which you might either accept or decline.

Memorize these words carefully and then close this window.

As casually as she could, Rebecca looked around, but nobody else in the lecture hall was paying her any attention whatsoever. The true source of this message, if it lay within the room, was not inclined to give itself away. Maybe, she thought, it had been sent from that office down the hall. For wasn't this likely to be a ploy on the part of Colonel Havers – designed to flush her out? She could hear his words now:

You're not going to last are you, Kent. I give you one month before you try pulling off a smart-ass move like some avenging fury.

Perhaps he was trying to prompt this same action in her now and have his theory proven correct? Going after Radan's remaining students, starting with herself first of all. In that case, the best policy was to ignore this approach. But of course, there was no way of knowing in advance if this was true, and the problem with living to fight another day was that the rules of engagement were becoming ever less favourable. The odds of a successful escape attempt were set to keep on decreasing, especially with Jacob out of the picture, and could she really reconcile herself to a lifetime spent at PROPS, doing the bidding of the military?

At that point, Rebecca stopped with these thoughts and started considering the instructions before her. Committing them to memory, just in case...

After the lecture, Rebecca returned to the canteen for dinner. Here she tried lending herself the appearance of normality, as best she could, while trying to figure out her response. So if it wasn't Havers, then who? Chuck White? Professor Radan? If the offer was genuine then its sender was not without certain powers (more than Rebecca herself possessed), but could these be translated into decisive actions as well?

After dinner she was escorted back to her room. Straight away Rebecca looked over at the alarm clock on her bedside table, the only device left that hadn't been confiscated the day before. 6:12 pm it read. Over and over again, she turned and looked at its face. It seemed to be moving at great speed, hunting down the minutes, bringing the moment of truth ever nearer.

6:22. 6:36. 6:48. 6:57...

Still the time flew by, accompanied by her tremendous indecision, with Rebecca remaining unsure as to what she would or would not do. Then, as the alarm clock struck 7pm, she commanded herself to get up, walk straight over to the door, and try the handle carefully. In this way, Rebecca discovered that the room was indeed unlocked, just as predicted in the message. She opened the door tentatively, enough to view the corridor to her right, and see that the coast was clear in this direction. Now came a greater gamble. Rebecca opened the door further again so that she might scan the other way, darting her head round the door-jamb. This portion of the corridor was empty also. She examined those nearby cameras stationed high up on the walls and saw that they were all configured in her favour, turning a blind eye to the progress she might make. Exactly as promised.

Almost before she knew it, Rebecca was closing the door behind her, moving clear of the room, following these instructions to the letter. Giving herself over to this wild leap of faith. She kept to the centre of the passageway and moved towards its far end. There was no sound at all, other than her own delicate footsteps, but such were Rebecca's nerves that this silence felt temporary, as if it was only a prelude to a total lockdown and the sound of all the building's alarms ringing out.

She reached the end of the corridor, turned left, kept on going. The thirty metres before her felt endless, impossible, but still she walked forwards, fighting off the temptation to break into a run. And then it was there on her left, level with her own body. A door labelled SUPPLIES. Rebecca opened the entrance up, slipped inside, closed the door with care. She turned around. The room was dim, deep, containing long rows of metal shelving. These were stacked with detergent bottles, cleaning fluids, packs of toilet roll. As Rebecca tried to steady her breathing, Radan stepped into the open at the far end of the room and it was then she knew that the proposal was genuine. The Professor was risking everything as well.

"Rebecca," he nodded, stepping towards her.

"Why here and not my room?" She said.

"Although I have taken care of the video surveillance,

I believe it may also be compromised by several listening devices of which I am not aware."

"OK. What is it you have to tell me?"

"Today I have created an executive order of my own devising. A phantom decree which appears to have been issued from way up on high and thus supersedes all base authority. At least for a short while. It states that a plane is currently waiting for me at the designated runway, bound for Washington DC, and a rendezvous with Graves at Cyber Command. Of course, it won't withstand any kind of close inspection from Havers, this deception, but it might last until dawn if fortune decides to favour us. Time enough to reach the nearest domestic airport and clear US borders."

"With what documentation?"

"That's been taken care of. I will explain this in time, should you decide to proceed." He looked at his watch. "You now have a further seven minutes to make this decision before the lock turns on your room and the cameras return to their normal setting. Of course I can offer you no kind of guarantee. Not even that we will make it off this base in one piece. And afterwards, they're going to throw everything they've got at this situation. This will make you public enemy number one. Dead or alive, it will make little difference to them how your capture occurs. Regardless of where you go, they will be hot on your trail. For these reasons, I will understand if you prefer not to go ahead, but I will trust you not to say anything to anybody. Once I put this into effect, there is no turning back."

"Of course I'm going ahead. You know that already, Professor. Let's not waste any more time."

He nodded. "Good. The odds are stacked firmly against you, but with your gifts, it is not impossible. And 'not impossible' is all we have to work with right now." He took a pair of cuffs from his pocket. "Turn round. I'll need to put these on. I've already been cleared on the way in here by the Staff Sergeant, but these are for sake of appearance. It should be a formality to get you out of this building. After that, we will have to wait and see."

CHAPTER 23

They went out into the corridor and returned the way Rebecca had come, passing by her sleeping quarters. Then they took another left and rounded the last corner, Rebecca walking a little ahead of Radan. Her heart was again in her mouth as she looked over at the Sergeant on duty, sat behind his desk, although he did not return her stare as yet. Radan strode forward with purpose, a hand on the small of Rebecca's back, and then steered her to a temporary stop, level with the soldier. "Thank you, Florio. And goodnight." At this, the Staff Sergeant looked up and nodded blankly at the Professor. Considered Rebecca for a moment. Then, without further interference, the two of them were permitted to leave the building behind.

Directly outside, in the gathering dusk, a grey Ford Explorer XLT was parked up. Radan opened the back door for Rebecca to get inside. "Stay down on the floor. This should provide you with adequate cover on account of the tinted windows. There is no reason for them to search the vehicle itself."

"You think?"

"I concede that this part of the plan lacks a certain finesse, but it is nevertheless the best option that we have."

"So you're driving yourself out of here without any military escort?"

"Yes. In theory I may still come and go as I please. This is not an impossible scenario."

"No. Maybe not. But that doesn't make it altogether likely either."

"If you prefer to stay, I will try and return you to your quarters now."

"That's not what I'm saying. I'm just pointing out that we could do with some luck here."

"Yes," said Radan. "I agree."

Rebecca got down on the floor of the vehicle and stretched herself flat, looking up at the Ford's roof. "And your hack is watertight?" she asked.

"It is. My main concern is with the Duty Sergeant's sixth sense."

"Better hope he doesn't have one then."

Radan closed the door on her, climbed up into the driver's seat, closed that door as well. He turned the key in the ignition and the engine started up first time. Then he depressed the handbrake and drove off towards the only road leading out of PROPS and the security presence which stood in their way.

The Professor slowed the car as the main gates approached, and then brought it to a standstill before their thick, reinforced steel. There were four armed guards stationed out in the open, either side of the barrier. Off to the right, a pale concrete bunker with a single wide window, allowing it a perfect view of all traffic in and out. After twenty seconds, another soldier walked out of this station and approached the car. Radan wound the window down for his inspection. "Sergeant Baines."

"Professor," Baines nodded.

"I have a flight to catch shortly to Washington. My presence is required at Cyber Command."

The Sergeant nodded again slowly. Repeatedly. "Right. And you have a P20 to confirm this?"

"I have." Radan's hand went into the breast pocket on his shirt and he removed the security card in question.

"I'm just going to run this by the system for confirmation, Professor. Shouldn't take a minute."

"Of course. I would expect nothing less."

Baines made his way over to the bunker again. Once inside, Radan could see him through the glass, his face illuminated by the glow of a large monitor. He had no doubt inserted the executive order into the NDT module and was now awaiting the green light. As Baines leaned over the device, he looked up again and towards Radan's vehicle. Radan instinctively pushed his glasses up onto the bridge of his nose.

A minute went by. Then the Sergeant stood up straight, moved away from the desk, stepped back out of the station into the warm night air. He walked over to the car, the card in his hand, and returned it to Radan. "OK, Professor. Have yourself a safe flight."

"Thank you." The gates immediately began to open outwards. When they were fully extended, Radan pressed down on the accelerator, nice and slow, and drove clear of them.

There were a couple of outer perimeters still to navigate. Twice more, the Professor was stopped, although here it was enough for him to state his business clearly to see him waived through. After that the two of them were free of the PROPS facility and could access the open road.

CHAPTER 24

Jacob did not know how long he'd slept, but by the time he climbed down from the single bed he felt well-rested. First he went over to the washbasin in the corner of the room and ran the cold tap. Cupped his hands underneath it and splashed the water into his face. There was no plug attached to the basin and Jacob saw that the fixture itself was all of one piece, sculpted from the wall. It was the same wherever he looked. Few joins. No electric sockets. A design philosophy which made for a smooth, inescapable space. Next he tried moving the small table and single chair away from the centre of the floor, but found that they were both fixed to it. Then Jacob looked up and saw that there were small cameras mounted in all four corners of the high ceiling. They were already tracking his movements, few as these were, as he explored the room's boundaries.

Half an hour passed and then the door to the cell opened. First to enter was the same huge guard who had led him there yesterday. Garcia. He was carrying a metal tray, breakfast sat on top of it. Next came a small man in his early sixties with large metal glasses, a grey beard, the overall look of an ageing scientist. This second figure walked over to where Jacob was stood, his right arm extended. "Good afternoon, Jacob. My name is Stanley Watson and I am the Senior Manager here at Grey-3." A smile accompanied the greeting and it did not look unkind nor seem like a cruel joke. Conflicted as Jacob was, he shook the offered hand.

The guard set the tray down on Jacob's table. Watson now lifted up the cover on the dish and revealed a steaming bowl of oats with bananas diced into the meal. He ducked down, smelled the aroma, and nodded approvingly. "There's no reason for us not to feed you well. Not under these circumstances. Which is why I ensure that all my wards are well catered for." Now Watson looked up and over at him again. "That said, I have a job to do here, Jacob. I'm not going to make unnecessary threats, but I do think it only fair to let you know what you're in for. I'm free to disclose anything and everything to you because there's no way you're ever getting off this rock. That's the plain truth of the matter." He sounded casual, almost friendly.

"Where is this place?"

"Oh, you're on a very very remote volcanic island set down in the South Atlantic, not so far from Antarctica. A place we've rented from another friendly power for the next hundred years. As for Grey-3, well it's the lockdown of the future. A research and development facility as much as anything...You know how many other long term residents we have here, Jacob?"

"Obviously not."

"Twenty-six at present. That's for a facility measuring 22,000 square metres, 2,500 miles from any other landmass, and costing approximately one billion dollars a year to run. Now what do you think that might mean, in real terms, for yourself?"

Jacob shook his head, feeling his anger begin to surge.

"Well, take your own wing, D1, for example. This is where we retain a small handful of wrong-headed individuals with truly extraordinary gifts. You messed up spectacularly, as I understand it, and then you messed up spectacularly again. Now we get to treat you like a scientific curiosity and spend a whole lot of time exploring your ins and outs, right down to a sub-molecular level. And if you're as bright as I've been led to believe then I think we're in for some truly fascinating discoveries."

"And when do I get to see a lawyer?" It was a hopeless question and Jacob knew this in advance.

"As I think you're aware, Jacob, you've already forfeited any such right."

"Look, I know you don't want to hear this, but I've been stitched up completely. I can prove this to you. Really I can. All I need is access to a computer for one single day."

Watson nodded, as if he'd only been waiting for this appeal. "You should know that things are going to go a lot easier for you here if you accept your situation for what it is."

"Then give me one single hour. That's all I'm asking."

Watson shook his head sadly. "You've got the rest of the day to yourself, Jacob. Take it easy, relax, put your feet up. Tomorrow morning your first assessment begins."

CHAPTER 25

Rebecca got up from the floor of the Explorer and sat down on the back seat as the 4×4 bumped along. She looked out the window into the pitch-black night. It appeared to be an old logging road they were driving along, lit up by the Ford's full beams, flanked by enormous pine trees. "So you know where we are exactly?"

"The wilds of North Carolina," Radan answered, "which is why we're headed for Atlanta. The nearest regional hub. After that, Rebecca, it's up to you."

"Sounds like you're not coming with me, Professor."

"That is correct. For one thing, there is no way for me to breach customs, given my appearance." Here Radan allowed himself a wry smile. "Imagine what would happen to my fake ID, no matter how competent the forgery. The likelihood is that they would check, double-check, and check again, and would still not be satisfied until they'd identified its flaws. A gentleman of Middle-Eastern appearance leaving the country on a sudden impulse. This is not an easy sell. But you. You are a happy young American student off to see the world. This is not such an alarming proposition."

"So there's a passport which spells this story out?"

"In the first pocket of the laptop bag. On the seat opposite." As Rebecca leaned over and searched it out, Radan continued. "This bogus document is of the very highest specification. It boasts a new technology capable of combating all facial recognition software in use at worldwide border controls. Also, I've erased your real details from all relevant data-banks. Until Cyber Command figures this out and re-instates your true profile, you're not going to get flagged at the airport. The only way anybody is going to recognise you in the short-term is by comparing your face with a photographic image. Of course, it is best if you keep a low profile as well. But this should, with luck, see you through to your next destination. After that, any advantage will dwindle quickly."

Rebecca read the name on the passport out loud. "Carol Keane."

"That's right. Studying at UCLA state. Now off on a foreign adventure. On the other seat, there is a backpack for you to put on, with a few changes of clothes inside."

"And there's a computer in here?" Rebecca lifted the laptop bag up.

"Yes. A fairly undistinguished spec, but I have prepared it as best I can. There is no way for you to take a PROPS machine through customs. It would arouse far too many suspicions. However, I have included a first class operating system and a range of software which I have designed myself over a number of years. I've also included backdoor access to all major government networks, including that of PROPS, which should permit you to stay abreast of what's going on. Also, what little I know about Jacob's current whereabouts is contained on the machine."

She looked up, stared at the Professor's eyes in the rear-view mirror "So you do know where he is?"

"I don't have the exact co-ordinates, but I believe the facility is somewhere in the South Atlantic, away from global shipping lanes."

"And what will happen to him there?"

"I believe they will subject Jacob to a range of invasive procedures. Procedures that will damage him irreparably. I can only guess at the time frame, but I suspect you do not have long to act if that is what you choose to do."

"And is there really a chance that I can save him?"

"The question is incalculable. There is no way of knowing this in advance."

Rebecca paused before replying. "And what's going to happen to you?"

Radan flicked the question away with a dart of his hand. "I am long past caring about myself. This way I get to resign my post by doing an honourable thing. There are much worse fates, Rebecca. Many of them I have already experienced..." Radan broke off from talking, surprised by a sudden sharp bend. He stepped on the brakes and the Explorer skidded around the curve, barely keeping to the road. "In all likelihood," he continued, "I'll be discovered before too long and then questioned by any means necessary. For that reason, it's best you don't tell me anything about your itinerary. But you do have an idea of where to go?"

"Yes."

"Then I suggest you try booking your flight now. There is a wallet in the same pocket as the passport. There you will also find a credit card and security details."

Rebecca took the wallet out, removed the laptop, placed it on her knees. She booted up the Dell machine, opened the Firefox browser, and accessed that list of available flights out of Atlanta airport to see if her only idea was a practical one. There she found what she was looking for and checked its precise details. Then she peered between the front seats at the clock on the dashboard. "How long till we reach Atlanta?"

"I'm not exactly sure. Between one and two hours."

"We could do with making that closer to one."

"You've got a flight to catch?"

"I certainly hope so."

Radan put his foot down on the pedal.

"Can I ask you why you're really doing all this, Professor? I'm grateful to you of course, but from your end, it looks like madness."

He nodded. Took his eyes of the road for a second to look back at her. Went into his shirt pocket and took out the box of Bahman cigarettes and a plastic lighter.

"You know I am from Iran?"

"Yes."

"What else do you know?"

"Nothing. But there were no shortage of wild guesses back at PROPS."

Radan lit the cigarette he'd removed, took a big drag on it, followed by a long exhalation. "Growing up I also had a special gift which was recognised by my country's authorities. So much so that by the time I reached university age I was singled out and granted one-to-one tuition with the most eminent of our computer scientists. It was also at this time that I met Hediyeh, a fellow student at Tehran University, and fell deeply in love with her...

"Nine months later I was withdrawn from the university and selected for involvement in my country's nuclear program, defending it from the cyber attacks of hostile nations. A task I performed with notable success. So much so that my profile grew as a result, both inside Iran and outside its borders. With this notoriety came fresh danger from both sides: if it wasn't an assassination attempt by foreign-backed operatives, then it was the regime itself I had to worry about, fearful of my abduction. And so, reluctantly, I had to balance my great love for Hediyeh against the serious threats she faced by staying with me.

"After weeks of reflection, I broke off the engagement at great emotional cost to myself and my fiancé. I did what I believed to be the sensible thing and crushed my soul in the process. A year later, Hediyeh became engaged to another man, and shortly afterwards she married him. Afterwards I tried with limited success to put this same knowledge out of my mind and my heart.

"By now my parents were dead. My sister had left the country. And I had estranged myself from all close friends, cutting myself off from everybody, preparing the way for my own departure. Shortly afterwards, I managed to make contact with a CIA operative and a plan was put into effect which saw me smuggled out of the country over the Northern border with Turkey, and then on to the USA.

"For a couple of months after arriving in the US, I enjoyed those new freedoms afforded to me, and the exciting new work I was asked to perform, and yet I had made a great mistake. Because I desired with all my heart and soul to forget the past, I'd somehow convinced myself that the Interior Ministry would follow suit. In fact, nothing was further from their minds and after I defected, they returned to my personal history and examined it with enormous care, looking for a way to repay me for my betrayal. It was a month after I arrived in America that a number of images were sent on to me by email. Of Hediyeh's dead body. I thought I had grieved for her already, in giving up her hand in marriage, but here, at last, was the true cost of my actions..."

Rebecca could think of no adequate reply and so she said nothing. Radan kept to this silence as well, his concentration given over to driving at the optimum speed, aware that they needed to put as much distance as possible between themselves and PROPS in the time left to them.

Fifteen minutes later, they saw light up ahead, and shortly afterwards they hit a regular road. Another five minutes and they passed a large sign for Atlanta. The forest began to fall away entirely. They'd reached Highway 19.

*

It was nearing 9pm when they reached their destination. Radan stopped the vehicle a couple of miles from the airport, outside its surveillance perimeter, not wanting the Explorer to be registered on camera. He turned in the seat and offered Rebecca his hand. "I wish you the very best of luck."

Rebecca took his hand and nodded. "Thank you, Professor Radan. For everything"

"Please. Call me Farid."

"OK, Farid. Much obliged."

Rebecca got out of the car and lifted the rucksack onto her shoulders. Then she picked up the laptop bag in her right hand. Radan watched her for a few seconds, then he turned the Ford around and shot away.

The professor drove for another half an hour, keeping to the edges of the city, looking about him all the while. Finally he pulled the Explorer over onto a deserted lot, a battered sign still hanging overhead from two concrete posts: Bernard Sanders Used Vehicles. This one-time forecourt now reduced to urban scrub, strewn with rubble.

Here Farid parked the car, climbed out, and walked away from the Explorer with the door to it open and the keys still in the ignition. He kept on for a mile and a quarter until he spotted a small neighbourhood bar. Then the Professor crossed the road towards it, pushed the creaking door open, and stepped inside. The place was almost empty. He walked over to the counter and tried engaging the morose man stood behind it, a dish towel draped over his left shoulder.

"I would like a bottle of liquor," Radan said.

"To take out of here?"

"Yes."

The man shook his head firmly. "We don't do that."

"Please. Here is fifty dollars." Radan placed the money flat on the bar.

The barman looked at the money. "We don't do that here for fifty bucks."

Farid dropped another fifty on top.

"How does Jim Beam grab you?" The barman asked, moving over to the well-stocked shelf

"Yes, fine, thank you. And where is the nearest motel from here...?"

Back outdoors, Farid followed the barman's directions to the letter and ten minutes later he was there in the reception foyer of the Excelsior Motel, giving the night manager a week's money in advance; paying for his room with cash upfront.

CHAPTER 26

There were a number of taxis heading away from the airport, most of them occupied, but after a minute Rebecca managed to flag an empty one down. The driver leaned over and opened the window on the passenger side. "Where you going?"

"The same way you just came."

At this he snorted. "That's no kind of fare." But with time pressing, she sought to reach a compromise by taking a twenty dollar bill from her wallet and offering it to the man. The driver regarded the note, then unlocked the door from the inside, nodding his agreement. "That we can do."

Five minutes later Rebecca was entering Hartsfield-Jackson airport, Concourse E. She could see a row of Delta Airlines check-ins across the hall and over to her left, and as she got closer to them, Rebecca recognised that two of these were clearly marked for Dublin: DL176. 21:45hrs. Stopping twenty metres shy of the desks, she engaged one of three automated machines stationed there, touching the menu screen, typing her details in with all due speed. Then, with the ticket printed out, she hastened over to the one desk which was free and took out her passport in advance of its very first test.

All Rebecca could do now was put her faith in this forged document and not add to its workload by acting out of turn. She needed to keep out of the way – be low-key, quiet, polite, reserved – and allow the fake to speak for itself. As for her appearance, the clothes she had on were standard PROPS issue, but there was nothing about her white t-shirt or jeans to suggest an escaped felon.

The female rep at the desk was all smiles. She took the ticket and passport from Rebecca's hand and referred them both to her internal system. Nothing in the woman's behaviour changed as the documents were logged in, nor was there any evidence of a suspicious delay. Instead, the large bag was swiftly tagged and checked through. "Don't worry, I'll see this gets aboard," she said. Then the rep gave Rebecca her documents back. "You better hurry. Gate closes in fifteen."

Rebecca turned and walked as fast as she could to customs control, clearly signposted, and reached it inside of two minutes. There were a couple of sizeable queues already formed, gradually being processed, and the sight of them filled Rebecca with dread. She showed her passport again at the top of the line and got it back from the tall male official stationed there after a brief glance. Here, fortune was on her side, as a third line had just opened up, and the same official, acknowledging the nearness of her own flight, directed Rebecca straight towards it.

Rebecca emptied out her pockets. Took off her shoes. Placed both of these in a tray.

"You have a laptop in there? Asked another customs official, alluding to Rebecca's bag, still on her shoulder.

"I do."

"Then remove it for me please. This should have been done already. I would advise you in future to pay attention to the signs all around you." The woman gestured to a large instruction sign on a stanchion to her left. Clearly stating the rules.

"Sorry."

Rebecca took the laptop out and the disgruntled official carried it off and over to a table containing a separate large X-ray machine. Now Rebecca was gestured forward by a different official and passed through the metal detector. She was allowed to advance, without a body search, and collect her belongings once more. The tray containing her shoes and empty bag had already cleared the inspection point and she picked these up and slipped the shoes back on. But with the laptop there was a delay.

Rebecca turned and saw that a customs official was still scrutinising the computer's insides, in no hurry to conclude this examination. Although Professor Radan had explained that the special operating system was carefully hidden away behind the Windows 8 front end, maybe there was something else about the machine which would strike them as odd. Some technical quirk which had escaped the Professor's attention? Rebecca looked up at the wall clock. She had five minutes to make the gate. And yet, knowing that any show of impatience would be catastrophic, Rebecca made a point of looking impassive, trying to retain what calm she had.

Shortly afterwards, the customs official sauntered over to Rebecca and handed her back the Dell laptop. "Thanks," Rebecca said, squeezing out a thin smile. Then she stuffed the machine into her laptop bag and broke into a run, desperate to make Gate E12 in time.

"Last call for Carol Keane. This is the last boarding call for Miss Carol Keane."

It took Rebecca a moment to realise the announcement related to herself. She upped her pace again and when she saw the gate from a distance, began waving her documents in the air.

"I'm here! I'm here! Hold on!"

Rebecca stopped before the desk, handed over her ticket and passport, and again the passport did its job and went unnoticed. "Just in time, Miss Keane," said the Delta representative. It was not an unfriendly assessment.

Clearly this didn't count as a low-profile approach, but here she was anyway, striding down the gangplank, clutching her documents, the laptop bag swinging against her right hip. Rebecca reached the threshold of the aircraft, boarded it, and the stewardess waiting there threw her a look. "I know, I know, I'm sorry," Rebecca said. She was directed to her seat, 7A. Put her bag in the hold above, sat down and fastened her seatbelt.

Now Rebecca was bound for a continent she had no prior knowledge of. All she had to go on was two lines of a rural address, committed to memory, with no way of knowing if it still held good. And yet this remained, by some distance, the best option she could think of. Rebecca simply had to hope her deception could hold firm for another seven and a half hours. Time enough for her to arrive in Dublin and clear customs there as well.

After that, she would need to find the one person whom she still trusted because he, in turn, no longer trusted anyone else.

CHAPTER 27

As soon as the Boeing 757 had reached a cruising altitude, and the seatbelt signs had been switched off, Rebecca stood up, stepped into the aisle, and took the laptop bag down. The seat next to her was unoccupied and so she left the empty bag there after removing the machine and plugging its lead into the power socket. One of the benefits of flying first class.

While on the road with Radan, Rebecca had made a couple of quick calculations. She'd checked an up-to-date plan of the plane's available seating and noted that while cabin class was heavily subscribed to, there was still plenty of space up front in first. And so she'd reserved one of these costly seats – as it allowed for considerable privacy, not to mention Wi-Fi access – knowing she had a host of important work to do. Maybe this was not how most students travelled, and jarred slightly with her cover story, but there was no reason why Carol Keane couldn't have been blessed with rich parents. Rebecca laughed inwardly at this thought. As for herself, nothing could have been further from the truth.

While the Dell booted up, a stewardess approached her and offered Rebecca a menu, but she politely declined. "I'd be obliged if you just brought me a large mug of coffee," she said. "Strong as you possibly can."

With the computer on the fold-down desk turned

towards her, away from the aisle, Rebecca went into MS Word and followed Radan's earlier instructions. A split second later Windows went down and the system reverted to its command line interface. Then it began executing a series of directives at high speed, reeling through countless lines of code and installing this new shell on the laptop. The coffee arrived as Rebecca kept her eyes on this process and thanked the stewardess distractedly. Then she looked up before the attendant could depart. "Actually, is there any way you might be able to get me a jug of coffee as well?" Rebecca asked. "That way I can help myself and leave you in peace."

"Let me see what I can do," the stewardess answered. While she was gone, the program finally finished loading and sprang to life. An operating system devised by Radan himself. Rebecca took a few minutes to admire its overall design, assess its capabilities, and then she looked at those two named directories in the dead centre of the screen. PROPS and WYLDE, they read.

No doubt Radan had arranged them this way to focus her mind and concentrate her thoughts on these couple of options. There were only two ways to go about this task: either she could start by trawling through the PROPS system, investigating the prime suspects in an effort to unmask the true culprit; or she could strive to somehow make contact with Jacob and try springing him from his captivity. Both deeds seemed highly unlikely, bordering on the impossible. Furthermore, it was difficult to see how she could engage in either line of inquiry without alerting hostile elements to her presence. At some point her own position would surely be revealed.

This realisation led Rebecca to consider her third option. That of admitting defeat in advance and simply disappearing from sight, leaving Jacob to his fate. But that did not sit right with her at all and it went against how she defined herself. Also, Rebecca wanted to be reunited with the young Englishman and find out if they truly belonged together. After everything, she decided, it was a risk worth taking.

The longer Rebecca considered the two directories, the more she favoured WYLDE as her starting point. Realising that what she needed to do, if they were to have any chance of success, was to empower Jacob himself and bring his gifts into play. If she could somehow get a device into his hands then there was no telling what he might be able to achieve.

Her mind made up, Rebecca opened the directory and clicked open the first of its seven files. It was a short intelligence briefing, originating with the Russian Security Services, and then translated into crude English. Unfortunately it offered little more than a vague overview of the facility where Jacob was being held, containing written descriptions of the island on which it was situated. The second and third files were little better – largely the same thing – only this time they came courtesy of the Chinese authorities. Here there were a couple of satellite images attached as well, but these were far from illuminating, displaying a great black asymmetrical structure against a backdrop of stark white. Certainly neither military power had penetrated the detention facility or made inroads into its operating system. There were no schematics on view. She did not even know the place's name. It felt to Rebecca like she was clutching at straws.

The last four files in the directory were also all of one type, but thankfully a lot more promising, sourced direct from the US Military. Here Rebecca found a large number of personnel records in full, scanned exhaustively. Names, addresses, backgrounds, personality evaluations. Everything was there in alphabetical order. And while there was no definite link to the detention facility, it was clear from the job titles on display that these people had been assigned to some vast, anonymous prison.

This had to be the staff roster.

There was a huge amount of data to sift through, but out of all the available information, this was definitely Rebecca's best shot.

The jug of coffee arrived, courtesy of the flight attendant, although Rebecca didn't even notice it being set down on the table. She had already started in on the first of these records, belonging to Brian Abrams. A Grade 3 Security Officer. Poring over his biography, running a background check of her own devising, referring the man's details to various databases on the lookout for any glaring contradictions. Something, anything, to arrest her in her tracks. An irregularity to pounce on.

Time flashed by and still Rebecca had nothing to show for it. The clock on the laptop's display, set to European time already, read 5.20 am. They were scheduled to touch down in Dublin inside of five hours. Worse still, an enormous tiredness was catching up with her now, refusing to respond to those refills of coffee from the jug. Also, the plane began to experience heavy turbulence. It shook the cabin violently and caused her laptop to slide around. In response, she was forced to cradle the machine with one arm while continuing with her tasks. For Rebecca, this stormy weather felt like a reflection of where she found herself mentally, adding to her growing sense of unease.

Ten minutes later, she came upon the personal details of an Executive Surveillance Technician called Davies Emery. And something about his profile caused a flag to go up in her mind. It was too perfect and squeaky clean, this background, as if his life had been carefully mapped out in advance, and Emery had found a way of keeping to this map without a single deviation. Something about it reminded Rebecca of those identities she used to pull together for herself in order to establish another fresh start.

At once she began to cross-reference Emery's personal history against those institutions he claimed to have attended in the past, and soon enough Rebecca discovered a curious lack of credible backstory. Neither his alleged high school, Homestead, nor his college, Reed, showed any sign of his ever being in attendance. In fact there was no active sign of Davies Emery anywhere online, prior to six years before.

Rebecca went down to the program menu and brought up the FBI database, installed by Radan. Then she ran a facial software program, comparing the impressions of Emery's face with those of countless others known to the governmental agency. Thousands upon thousands of them. Many minutes passed and Rebecca was starting to lose hope when a match occurred. The same face appeared on the left side of the screen, next to the image she had of Davies Emery. This second photograph had been taken a good few years earlier, but it definitely belonged to the same man. A man whose name was given here as Raymond Lowe. Without skipping a beat, Rebecca started to read the associated file and learned the story of this transformation.

It turned out that Lowe had been part of a gang working out of Pittsburgh, finally brought to book in 2005 on several counts of computer fraud, wire fraud, and possession of unauthorized access devices. And that Davies Emery was the identity which had been granted to him in exchange for testimony against his fellow conspirators. Also, between Lowe's willingness to co-operate, and his considerable technical gifts, the agency had offered him complete immunity from prosecution.

It was undoubtedly a breakthrough, this discovery, but Rebecca needed even more specifics, including some way to make contact with the man. And even if she could find a way to get in touch, Rebecca also had to decide upon the best method of targeting him. She would have one chance, and one chance only, to make her threat count.

CHAPTER 28

It was Garcia, the same muscular guard as before, who came into his cell the next morning. Jacob was already dressed, lying back against his pillow, trying to prepare himself mentally for whatever lay ahead. Now he lifted his legs around and sat up. "No breakfast today?"

"You'll be able to eat this afternoon. Right now you have a doctor's appointment."

Together they left the cell behind and walked along the eerily silent corridor, with no noise emanating from any corner of this angular space. As they passed the first bronze-coloured metal door, Jacob asked, "So who's my neighbour?"

"I wouldn't know," Garcia answered. "That's not my business. You are my only concern."

"So you're assigned to me especially?"

"That's correct."

"I suppose I should be flattered."

The giant shook his head firmly. "No. What you should be is concerned."

Jacob could see that Garcia had a non-lethal weapon affixed to his thick belt. Some kind of cutting-edge Taser by the look of it, although certainly he'd be capable of restraining Jacob in seconds using nothing else except his bare hands.

They stepped into an elevator which was already waiting for them, and this time headed upwards at speed. Thirty seconds later, the doors slid open and another corridor came into view and they duly entered it. This one put Jacob in mind of a hospital ward. It was sterile, spotless, and on either side there were rooms leading off from it, most of them visible through wide glass windows, allowing Jacob to stare inside briefly. What he saw was a menacing range of instruments whose exact function was not clear.

At the end of the corridor they came to a door with a small nameplate on it which read Dr Tim Billingsley. Here Garcia knocked twice.

"Come in," a voice answered from inside.

It was a long narrow room. At one end a glass-topped desk at which Billingsley himself was sat. He wore a white lab coat and had black, wiry hair. Sunken eyes. A serious demeanour. "Good morning," he said. "Take a seat."

They approached the table and Jacob sat down opposite while Garcia stood off to his right. "I understand you've spoken to Stanley Watson already and he's explained something of our procedures here?" Billingsley said.

"Not really," Jacob answered. "Only that you're going to treat me like a lab rat."

The doctor stared back at him coldly. "You must understand there is nothing to be gained here by being difficult. Of course, we're familiar with dramatic protests, but they will get you nowhere. That would only mean that we'd have to keep you sedated and then you get to wander around in a permanent daze. Before that happens, however, we're going to give you the benefit of the doubt and treat you in a civilized fashion."

"Not how I'd describe it," Jacob said.

The doctor ignored this further criticism. "So, I'd like to start by asking you about the fainting fit you experienced back at PROPS. In the Operations Room. Was that merely a pretence?"

Jacob shook his head.

"You're sure?"

"Yes I'm sure."

"And this had never happened before after similar mental exertions?"

"No."

"Well we'd better get to the root of it then."

"Listen. I'd prefer it if you stopped trying to sound like you're doing me a favour," Jacob said. "You're basically here to perform experiments on another human being. Nothing else."

"Who happens to be a foreign spy committed to the downfall of my own country, along with its foremost ally – the United States. As ethical dilemmas go, it's not the worst one I've ever faced."

"What you're saying is simply not true," Jacob told him.

But the doctor was already up out of his chair, gesturing to the far side of the room. Jacob stayed as he was for a couple of moments, and this was enough for Garcia to intervene. He stepped close to Jacob and lifted him up by his armpits like he was no weight at all.

Billingsley began his examination with a series of traditional tests. He shone a penlight in Jacob's eyes. Employed a stethoscope. Checked his reflexes. None of these techniques any different from those a regular doctor might use. But then, at the last, he had Jacob open his mouth and scraped matter from his cheek with a buccal swab. Gathering DNA. After placing the swab-head carefully into a collection tube, Billingsley looked back at Jacob "OK. Good. Now, if you'll stand up and follow me then you can see for yourself our new scanning unit. A machine which will become familiar to you in the coming days. This is where you'll be spending a great deal of your time."

Two doors down from Billingley's office, the three of them entered a rectangular room, brightly lit, dominated by a large bizarre object at its centre. It looked less like a piece of medical equipment than the hollowed out engine of a fighter plane, painted brilliant white, with a black surgical bed extending from it.

It was unlike anything Jacob had ever seen.

"You've heard of MRI scans?"

"Yeh."

"Well the principles here are similar. Only this allows us to go a step further and understand your physiology to a truly extraordinary degree. It's not going to hurt you in any way. Only detail exactly who and what you are." Billingsey stopped next to the scanner and put out his arm. "Now, if you'll place yourself up on the motorised bed, then we can make a start..."

Jacob stood there angry, anxious, tempted to act up. Then he became aware of Garcia rocking back and forth on his feet, as if warning him against it. Reluctantly, Jacob complied with Billingsley's wishes and lay himself flat against the surgical mattress. Out of the corner of his eye he watched as the doctor moved off in to a side room which was slightly raised. There he leaned over those instruments before him, looking like some recording technician in a musical studio making use of an editing suite. Behind Billingsley, Jacob could distantly make out row after row of blue monitor screens, no doubt waiting to examine every atom of his body.

The motorised bed began to move backwards and Jacob watched the bright ceiling above him until it disappeared from view, replaced by the inside of the scanner's chamber. He was completely engulfed now. It was dark to begin with, although Jacob could see that the inner surface was strangely globular, as if pebbled with thousands of tiny glass balls. A minute later, he detected the first stirrings of noise. It sounded like a whisper rotating across the scanner's circumference, quickly building up speed. Then, suddenly, the chamber lit up, with each of the miniature bulbs coming alive, creating a dazzling composition of blues and greens. Like thousands of fiery marbles given over to sequential patterning. It was a hypnotic spectacle and fearing that it would send him into a trance, Jacob closed his eyes tight, although still the light pulsed through his closed lids for minute after minute after minute. Bombarding his very being.

He could not be sure how long he spent in the machine, but it felt to Jacob like an hour. At the end of that time, the lights were cut off, the constant whispering ceased, and the motorised bed began its withdrawal from the chamber. As it came to a stop, Jacob saw that Billingsley was already standing there above him on his right hand side. "If you'll just stay as you are for a few moments longer…"

As Jacob remained in that position, he felt the doctor take hold of his left arm without warning and apply something to his skin. It felt like he'd been scratched with a sharp fingernail. In reply, Jacob raised himself up on his elbows, looked down at his forearm, and then back at the doctor. "What the hell was that?"

While the question still hung in the air, Jacob began to lose his focus, feeling increasingly light-headed. "Think of it as a lullabye," the blurred figure replied. And by the time Jacob realised what the Doctor meant by this, he had gone under completely.

*

When Jacob woke again he was back in his cell, wearing new clothes. A loose-fitting grey sweater and jogging bottoms. He felt groggy and his whole body tingled as if suffering from a case of pins and needles from head to toe. He remembered his last moments of consciousness. Billingsley grabbing his arm, employing some kind of sedative. After that, nothing at all.

It made for a hellish gap.

Jacob had absolutely no idea how long he'd been unconscious. It might have been thirty minutes. It could have been a full day. Time enough to conclude all kinds of sinister procedures. Now he tried rising to his feet slowly, but dizziness greeted him and Jacob dropped back down on his bed. With some effort, he took off his t-shirt and slipped out of his tracksuit bottoms. Then Jacob began checking his body for signs of surgery, using his fingers to check for stitching, scarring, or the like. To conclude this self-examination, he placed his right hand upon his head, feeling every inch of his skull. As far as Jacob could tell, no incisions had been made, and yet this hardly consoled him. This was just for starters. He had only reached day two of this endless captivity.

They would have their way with his entire organism until Jacob was all used up.

Chapter 29

It was the hovering presence of the flight attendant which woke Rebecca up. She immediately felt something close to panic, looking down at the laptop and the clock in its corner, realising that she'd been out for the best part of fifty minutes. It was 9:31 pm. They were scheduled to land in just under an hour.

The stewardess stood there, holding a hot towel with a pair of metal prongs. "I think maybe you could do with one of these?"

"You're not wrong." Rebecca leaned over, took hold of it, and pressed the towel into her face, trying vainly to reinvigorate herself.

"We'll be serving breakfast shortly." The attendant continued.

Rebecca shook her head. "I'll just take another coffee."

"Not even a croissant?"

"No. Thanks. I'm fine."

She looked back at the computer screen. The time back in North Carolina was now 5:33am. Exactly twenty seven minutes before the door to her room was scheduled to open so that her day there might begin. If Radan's plan had held firm – the tweaked surveillance feed, the fake authorisation – then maybe her disappearance still remained an unknown. Rebecca tried imagining the likely scenario back at PROPS if this was the case. Colonel Havers scrambling desperately into action on the strike of 6am, scouring every inch of the facility to begin with, enlisting every last member of staff. Praying that she was still somewhere within these strict perimeters. Then learning of Farid Radan's departure the evening before. The likely truth hitting Havers with the force of an ugly revelation. His career suddenly on the verge of going down the tubes.

In all likelihood, under these circumstances, he would try and buy himself a little time before bringing this to the wider attention of Cyber Command, and then, by extension, the whole US Military and Government. Only at that point would the hunt begin in earnest and stretch out worldwide. And hopefully by then Rebecca would have cleared Irish customs without any security alerts showing up on their system.

Detain This Woman. Whatever The Cost.

There was no doubt about it: her ability to make it out of Dublin unharmed was touch and go. And as the plane began its descent, Rebecca began to feel nauseous on account of this fact. There was no knowing what was waiting for her down there.

"Can you switch your laptop off now please," said the attendant, passing by again. "We're coming in to land."

*

After exiting the plane, the passengers off Flight DL176 filed across the runway and into the main airport complex. Rebecca felt like puking up her guts as she moved closer to her next moment of truth. Walking along the carpeted passageway among a crowd of fellow travellers, it was all she could do to keep her legs from giving out. At the far end of the long corridor a queue began to emerge, with four security booths beyond it. All too soon, Rebecca reached the back of this line.

As the queue moved along, in steady motion, Rebecca tried to get a sense of the customs personnel upfront: their faces, attitudes, differing approaches. Two of them were women. Two men. But before she'd had time to form much of an opinion, it was her own turn to face inspection.

She was beckoned over by a young woman with short blonde hair. Beautiful, stony-faced, unsmiling. Probably the worst fit out of those customs officers on duty. Rebecca stepped forwards, trying to make use of her weariness, passing herself off as one more tired traveller, worthy of pity whether she received it or not. "Morning," she said, using a hoarse voice.

The young officer ignored this greeting, took hold of the offered passport, and held it against the scanner inside her booth. Then she looked up at her screen to see what it told her. She read this information slowly from top to bottom.

"On vacation?" she asked, without looking back at Rebecca.

"Backpacking. Yes."

The young woman nodded again "On your own?"

"Yes."

"You don't know anybody in this country?"

"No. But I've heard that the Irish are a friendly bunch."

The woman looked away from the screen and gave Rebecca a hard stare. "That's what they say," she answered drily. Then she lifted up the document and gave her the passport back. As Rebecca walked away, she was close to tears. Tired and emotional. If minutes earlier she had struggled to keep down her nausea, now Rebecca tried hard to contain a wave of joy, knowing it to be premature.

She made her way to the baggage area and waited for her rucksack to show up. This was a calculated gamble.

There was nothing to stop Rebecca from leaving it there – certainly there was little of worth inside – only abandoning her luggage had the potential for raising the alarm. If not now exactly, then a little way down the line. On balance, it was better to collect it.

As Rebecca waited for the carousel to kick into action, she decided to use this time wisely by walking over to the Currency Exchange booth, only twenty feet away, to change the last of her US dollars. This transaction netted her 543 Euros in return. There was still the credit card at her disposal, and a pin number in the wallet allowing for ATM withdrawals, but Rebecca considered this a last resort. It was another potential trail for Cyber Command to follow. One more way to track her down.

Ten minutes later and her rucksack had still not arrived, unlike the luggage of most passengers who were already headed for the exit. Was this a delaying tactic? Rebecca felt a surge of paranoia, prickling the base of her neck. Maybe breaking news was just now hitting these shores, having an immediate impact? She tried not to look at those policemen on duty, armed and alert, but her eyes were drawn to them again and again. Just as Rebecca was on the verge of turning and departing in a panic, the bag finally dropped onto the conveyor belt. She walked round to where it had emerged from, took it off the belt, placed it on her back. Then she moved through that channel for those with Nothing To Declare.

Out into the arrivals lounge, Rebecca made directly for the exit. A mild grey morning awaited her, the sky spitting with rain. Fifty metres to her right, a row of taxi cabs was parked up. She went over to the head of the queue and approached the driver; a man in his fifties reading a paper called The Sporting Life.

"I want you to take me to County Leitrim. The town of Ballinamore," she said.

The man folded his paper and looked at her closely. "Well that's a fair way to go. You'd be better of spending the night in Dublin first and getting a train in the morning."

"I understand that it won't be cheap."

"No. Not by a long stretch."

"Look, I have two days in Ireland, and I need to see my friend. I don't have time to waste."

"To make it worth my while, I'd need to ask you for two hundred Euros," he said. "You might get it cheaper, I dare say, but then it's not a journey I'm all that keen on making. Told the missus I'd be back for lunch."

"Three hundred Euros then."

He shrugged, nodded. "OK. Get in. You've picked the right moment. Lucky for you, the whole economy is screwed."

CHAPTER 30

Rebecca climbed into the back of the green Vauxhall Astra, left the rucksack in one corner, and got out her laptop again. Then she plugged in that dongle which had been provided by Radan, praying that its reach was as global as he'd promised. The Dell machine brought up her operating system and the dongle immediately kicked into action, scanning the airwaves until it had found a local GNS network for Rebecca to piggyback.

So far, so good.

Immediately she returned to the dual identity of Raymond Lowe/Davies Emery and accessed his confidential FBI records. There was a Seattle address there on file and so Rebecca tried placing this in a search engine along with the man's new name. Although nothing relating to her target came back, there were several Google references to a women called Denise Emery, linking her to this same neighbourhood of Medina. The place where she was a chairperson of the Parents' Committee at the local nursery school. Also on the board of a tennis club.

Rebecca had no trouble in tracking this woman down on Facebook and began studying Denise's profile in depth. At the top of the page, there was an image of her in a large garden, two young children around her knees. One boy, one girl. Underneath, there were a large number of domestic updates up on her wall addressed to various friends, giving the impression of suburban bliss. And although there was no visible sign of any 'Davies Emery' on the page, there were a whole lot of mentions of him. Rebecca scanned through these quickly and it soon became clear that Denise was married to the man she needed to reach.

Thankfully, Denise Emery had left a recent message on her wall passing on her email address to a new acquaintance, and it was this Rebecca seized upon now. She went to the program menu and brought up those tools created by Radan. Chose one called CuSP. A password checker of the Professor's own devising which functioned as a dual purpose BIOS lock and C code tar file. She then set this program against Denise Emery's Yahoo account and it made light work of the challenge, cracking it inside three minutes.

Rebecca searched for those emails sent by the woman's husband and found a whole bunch of them, numbering 673. Racing through the first dozen, she pored over their contents, trying to form a quick impression. It turned out, for one thing, that this man was keeping the truth from his wife by claiming to be on assignment in the North Sea, working as a software controller on an oil rig. Lowe lamented his absence from home, complained about his work patterns, told Denise not to worry. The messages were all brief and tender and each time he concluded them by pledging his love to her and the children both.

Rebecca checked the dates and saw that there'd been plenty of back and forth correspondence inside the last seven days. The last one of his messages had been sent a mere four hours ago. So Lowe was accessing his gmail account from the furthest reaches of the South Atlantic, with or without the permission of his superiors. Either way, it didn't matter. She now had her entry point. It was only a question of how exactly the approach would be made and the best method for threatening him.

With this in mind, Rebecca brought up the FBI database again and considered Lowe's fellow gang members. The ones who had carried the can for him. All serving ten to fifteen up at Ryker's Island prison. At least three of these jailbirds had long rap sheets to their names and bore all the hallmarks of career criminals. Not men to be taken lightly. It was highly probable that they would appreciate an update on Lowe's whereabouts now that he'd dropped off the map and headed into the sunset. In all likelihood, revenge would be on the cards. Not that this was something Rebecca wanted to make happen, but it was one hell of a threat to wield. In a way, she did not like doing this. It returned her to a part of her life she'd just as soon forget. But there was no other choice. Rebecca needed leverage. It was time to drop a bombshell on Raymond Lowe and pray that he felt the heat.

Raymond Lowe,

I know all about your past and how you came to avoid jail and where exactly you are now. I also know everything about the new life you've set up for yourself with Denise and the kids out in Medina. Got all these details right here before me and thought I might send them out in a mailshot to Berrigan, Vallejo, and Spicer. See what they make of your happy home.

I am deadly serious here. You need to get in touch with me now or else I will make this nightmare come true. I want a secure number I can contact you on and I want it right away. If I don't hear from you in the next few hours, your whole family will be placed under threat.

Rebecca fired the message off and finally looked away from the screen, suddenly aware of the green surroundings flashing by. Dublin was long gone from view. They'd reached the countryside proper.

Chapter 31

It was 6.01am when Colonel Havers learnt that Rebecca Kent was missing from her room. Thirty seconds after the Staff Sergeant on duty had first opened it up and found it empty. After putting down the phone, Havers instantly picked up a quartz paperweight from his desk and launched it at a framed picture of himself hanging on the far wall. The glass front exploded on impact and then Havers heard his secretary outside, knocking on the door cautiously, asking if he was OK. Only then did he start to regroup mentally and think to sound the alarm.

The next logical step was to scour every last inch of the PROPS facility, and this task Havers oversaw, committing every last man and woman to the hunt, desperately hoping to find Kent hidden inside the grounds. But inside of the hour, he was forced to call the search off as the true picture began to emerge. The method of her escape, the identity of her partner in crime. At that point there'd been no alternative except to alert Cyber Command and inform Graves by video link. Not only was Kent absent, so – as it turned out – was Professor Radan.

"How long have they been gone?" Graves had asked him.

"Potentially eleven hours," Havers answered.

"Potentially?" It was a damning word, especially as Graves pronounced it.

Figuring that they couldn't have got far, Havers stayed on the phone, drawing on all his high level regional contacts, demanding word of any possible sightings. At this stage, it was not enough for him to be in the loop. He needed to somehow stay ahead of the game and steal a march on the rest of the hunting pack. Unless he was the one to recapture Kent and Radan, or else neutralise their threat, his career was as good as over.

The first breakthrough had come with the capture of the professor's Ford Explorer at 8.17am, turning up in the possession of two local youths. On learning of the vehicle's recovery, Havers had set off for Atlanta at once with his four most trusted lieutenants. The ones whose destinies were most closely bound up with his own. The ones who could be relied on to act decisively.

They were half an hour from the city limits when Atlanta's police chief lived up to his promise and called Havers back with the latest update.

Word of Radan's likely whereabouts. Maybe Kent's as well.

"You need to keep this under your hat for the next hour," Havers said.

"You've got yourself half of that," the chief answered. "And that's the best I can do."

Now Havers passed on the directions to his driver, and the man behind the wheel responded by maxing out the engine on the unmarked Chevrolet Caprice PPV. As they tore up the remaining miles in the direction of Carver Hills, the Colonel's mind was still trying to cover all the angles, think up a way to claw his reputation back.

Another fifteen minutes and the Chevy pulled to a

stop on Pollard Boulevard, having reached the Excelsior Motel. The time was 9.34 am.

"This needs to go down exactly like I said," Havers explained through gritted teeth.

Two of the four men nodded. All of them were untroubled by the Colonel's approach. They stepped out of the car into the morning sunshine, dressed in light fitting suits, their Sig-Sauer P229s holstered out of sight.

At reception, Havers asked the duty manager where Room 23 was. The motel employee, already informed of the soldiers' arrival, pointed outside through another open door. "Through the courtyard out back. Up the stairs. At the far end of the first floor."

The men removed their weapons, stepped out into the courtyard, and went up the stairs in two separate files. Havers followed after them, a short distance behind, brandishing his own Springfield.45 ACP.

The advance detail kept low, advancing swiftly along the first floor corridor. With a practised movement, they stopped outside the door to Room 23. One of the men tried its handle with great delicacy, turned and shook his head. Then they all shared in a flurry of hand signals. Describing their next actions.

One of the soldiers took a number of steps back, then he launched himself at the door and kicked at its centre with all his strength, so that it came away from its hinges at the first attempt. His three colleagues rushed through the newly made gap and fanned out, sweeping their weapons over the small room. Moving forwards steadily in a tactical formation. There was only one figure visible inside, sprawled on a crumpled bed. Three of the unit surrounded this person while the fourth made to secure the bathroom.

"Get up now, hands on you head! I said hands on your head now!"

But there was no word from the suspect. No movement either. He appeared to be out for the count.

Now Havers walked in and wasted little time in approaching the bed and poking the man with the barrel of his pistol. Then he jabbed him in the ribs and heard a distant moan from the depths of his throat. "Turn him over," Havers said. At this, two of his team came forward and rolled Radan over onto his back. This released an empty bottle of Jim Bean from underneath the Professor's body. The bottle dropped to the floor and rolled away. "He's wasted," said Havers. "Smells like a distillery. Have we got a bath in there?"

"Yep."

"Then get the water running and drag him inside." At the same time, Havers pulled a small notebook from his inside jacket pocket and scribbled on it furiously. Then he tore out the page and handed it to one of his team. "And I want these items from the nearest pharmacy now."

The soldier looked down at the list of medicines. "Heavy duty," he said.

"Your goddamn right it's heavy duty, Minnelli. This is a heavy duty situation."

CHAPTER 32

It was as they crossed the county border into Roscommon that Rebecca lost all GMS coverage. Up until then, as soon as one signal had faded, another had become more distinct, allowing her to make use of it. But now the dongle scanned in vain for an available frequency, frustrating her attempts to work online.

"I don't suppose you know of any Wi-Fi signals in this part of the world?" She asked. More hopeful than anything.

The taxi driver looked back at her through the rear-view mirror. "Can't say I do. But this is some wild country around here. You'd be better off expecting a few hiccups along the way."

"Right."

Seeing that she'd put her computer down for the moment, the driver continued. "Long time since you've seen this friend of yours?"

"About a couple of years," Rebecca said.

"He'll be pleased to see you then."

CHAPTER 33

At the age of seventeen, Rebecca had taken herself off across the US/Canadian border and rolled into Toronto. Travel hardened and not a little world weary as well. Or at least weary of those lowly, desperate corners where she'd ended up, time and again. She had the address belonging to a friend of a friend, good for a couple of nights. It was in the Kensington Market district of the city and here Rebecca pitched her sleeping mat that first evening.

Next morning she did as usual on entering a new town and tracked down the nearest internet café. It was a little way down the road, on the middle of Augusta Avenue, and went by the name of Blown Fuse. There she set to work.

At that time the money Rebecca lived off resulted mostly from 'spear phishing'. She would target a large corporation, sending out emails as if she belonged to its workforce, exploiting the vast size of the organisation and the lack of personal contact among staff. In this way Rebecca was able to gather enough information to access their systems at will and siphon off a little finance. This she issued to herself using a string of fake credit cards. At the same time Rebecca took every precaution, which was why she never went for the big score or stayed in any place long enough for authorities to get a fixed handle on her.

Having remained inside Blown Fuse for five hours in total, netting a few hundred bucks in the process, Rebecca went to settle up, but the guy behind the counter shook his head. "You're OK."

"What?" she answered.

"I said you're all right. You don't need to pay me." He was in his early thirties, skinny and bearded, with intense brown eyes.

"You think I'm that cheap?"

"How do you mean?"

"That's not the way into my pants, if that's what you think."

"And who says I'm even attracted to girls?" That question did a decent job of shutting her up. "If you must know, I have some experience of being where you are now."

"I see. And where is that exactly?"

"Pulling petty stunts in order to survive. A person with no fixed anything at all."

"And how would you know that I was doing any such thing?" Rebecca thought she'd been highly careful to cover her tracks.

"Because these are my premises and I have my good name to uphold. At least during regular hours." Then Jake cracked that great big smile of his which she would come to know so well and to cherish. The creases bunching up around his eyes. "Nice bit of work that, by the way, if a little rough around the edges."

"I only take from those who've got it to spare," Rebecca said.

"Well aren't you just the regular Miss Robin Hood."

The following day Rebecca started work at the café.

Jake was from Ireland himself – "way out in the sticks" – although he'd been 8 years in Canada now with a full residency to show for it. Gay or not, he showed no signs of hitting on her. However what Jake did do, day by day, was to grant Rebecca ever more license: thinking nothing of leaving her alone with the cash till, for one thing. Here was a man who almost instantly took her word on trust and had complete faith in her actions. It was a great novelty for Rebecca to be treated this way. More than that, a rare pleasure. It went against the grain of her childhood and an adolescence spent on the road, mostly fending for herself.

After another fortnight had passed, she moved in above the shop as well, where Jake kept an apartment of two floors. The top one resembled a storage dump, with old hardware components spread out across a number of rooms. But together they moved it all into one single corner and Rebecca made a home for herself in the space that they'd cleared.

On Jake's own floor he had a large office where he spent all his spare time. It was a chaotic nerve centre dominated by several interlinked computers. One day they'd be in working order and the next lying in bits. Or vice versa. It turned out that he liked building these machines for himself when he wasn't busy programming them, testing out their capabilities, or modifying their specs.

One night, a couple of weeks after she'd first moved in, Rebecca carried a coffee into Jake's sprawling domain and watched him in action from the doorway, sat at his cluttered desk. He was typing away furiously when she stepped closer to the screen, intrigued by the strings of code. "What is that you're doing?"

"Taking part in Inter-Alia. It's basically a wargame for hackers. A chance for me to compete against like-minded freaks." Jake turned and looked up at her as she placed the coffee down. "How'd you like to learn a thing or two?"

"Wouldn't say no."

"Then you'd better pull yourself up a seat."

That was the beginning of six months' worth of tutorials, with hardly any breaks. Yes she'd learnt plenty afterwards under Farid Radan, but this was a quantum leap forward in Rebecca's grasp of computing. Almost every night she'd accessed Jake's great store of knowledge, as well as sharing in a growing confidence as they gradually opened up to one another. Becoming the very best of friends.

Jake talked about his earlier life, working out in Silicon Valley for a succession of software start-ups. And about his growing dissatisfaction with this brilliant career. In the end he'd dropped out of one venture just as it was on the verge of becoming a household name, simply because it didn't interest him any longer. Then he'd left the whole industry behind. "More important things to do," Jake said.

"Like running an internet café?"

"You know and I know that's not the whole story."

"Of course I know. So why don't you fill me in?" Rebecca asked.

Jake sat there at his desk, stroking his beard with thumb and forefinger. "Alright." He'd already considered this possibility long and hard. Now he decided to come clean with her about his real ambitions.

In truth, Jake Brennan was in the middle of waging a one-man war against a company called Transom Oil. A Joint US/Canadian concern focusing its efforts upon the Athabasca oil sands up in Alberta. They were one of the pioneers of open pit mining and had also set up a new pipeline, running this heavy crude oil down to the States. More tellingly, their environmental record was diabolical and it was this which had made them Jake's sworn enemy. "If the devil were to hand out awards to the big petrochemicals, there'd be no shortage of nominees, but my money would still be on this company to sweep the board. They've taken despoilment to a whole new level."

"Have you been up there to Alberta to take a look?" she asked.

"What? And stand there waving a placard in front of a Caterpillar D12! No. This way I get to land my blows and then disappear only to double-back later."

"Couldn't you get others involved as well?"

"You have to be awful careful about trusting other people, Becca. There's a high degree of infiltration going on at present among all committed groups."

"Well you trusted me soon enough."

"That's because it was like looking in the mirror."

"Well maybe I could be of help then."

"I don't know that I want to see you implicated in this. The risks are enormous."

Rebecca thought this over quickly. "Listen Jake, if we're not family, me and you, then I'd say we're about as close to it as two one-time strangers can get."

He nodded sombrely "You won't hear any arguments from me on that score."

"Well then…"

Jake let his smile off the leash. "All right. Let's see what we can do."

It was a two pronged attack they worked on together over the next three months. To disrupt the extraction process itself, and also to wreak havoc on Transom's newly laid pipelines. Between these two measures, they started to achieve some notable results.

First they cracked the open-pit mining equipment, via its operating system, sabotaging temperature controls on the primary separation vessel. Then they launched a series of attack scripts on the pipeline sensors, knocking out those essential instruments for detecting any leaks. Altogether Transom lost nineteen production days during this time on account of Jake and Rebecca's efforts, kissing goodbye to two million barrels of oil.

It was during this early wave of success that Jake suffered his first fit. At least the first one that Rebecca had got to witness, although it would be nowhere near the last. One minute he was talking to her casually, the next he had slumped out of his chair and onto the floor. Jake's eyes tightly closed, lids fluttering rapidly like he'd entered deep sleep in an instant and was lost to a terrible dream.

For a minute and a half, Rebecca hovered above him with no idea what to do. And then Jake gradually came around, only to brush this incident off as "Nothing. Too much caffeine is all…"

In fact, it was the beginning of the end.

Even worse than the attacks themselves, Jake started to suffer an alarming side effect. His wariness regarding other people started to expand rapidly, to the point where he became ever more reluctant to go downstairs and supervise the café, believing there to be a number of government agents among the clientèle. This also meant, for all Rebecca's pleas, that he would not hear of visiting a doctor. By then Jake's suspicion of them, and everyone else for that matter, was starting to escalate and reach obsessive dimensions.

"You could do with a fortnight off from saving the world," Rebecca told him.

"Problem is these devils never rest. They're forever ticking over. And so the damage goes on an on and on."

As the fits became increasingly frequent, Jake's paranoia grew again. Until Rebecca was the only person excluded from his sweeping accusations. On top of this, he also gave in to a growing technophobia and would not touch any one of his computers, refusing to explain why.

By the time August arrived that year, Rebecca was less a partner in crime and more of a struggling nursemaid. She had no idea what to do next.

It was then, on the third Sunday in the month, that the door to their apartment was kicked through. The intruders were dressed in black, wielding automatic weapons, and refused to identity themselves even as Rebecca screamed for them to do so. At the same time Jake said nothing as they forced him to the floor. He looked pale, resigned, like he knew this moment had been coming and now he was travelling deeper into himself, seeking an impossible refuge there.

The two of them were blindfolded and taken off in two separate vans. Rebecca to be remanded in an anonymous cell block, an hour's drive from Toronto, where she was kept for a fortnight and interviewed at great length. Mostly by a man called LaRoux who said that he worked for the Canadian government.

At the end of this series of interviews, LaRoux broke it down for her: "We want you to do some computing for us, Kent. Show off your capabilities."

Rebecca nodded. "Go screw yourself."

"It's about the only chance you've got of retaining any freedom whatsoever. Pass this test with flying colours and you might just end up some place other than a high security jail."

But it was not her own fate Rebecca was thinking about when she finally agreed to the testing. Something had to be done for Jake.

For three straight days she was placed before a specially designed terminal and instructed to engage in various complex simulations, calling on all her speed of thought and intellectual powers. On the fourth afternoon, Roux shared with her the results. "You're a very very lucky girl. Seems like you got that all-important passmark."

Rebecca just stared at him.

"This means you'll be going somewhere shortly where they'll make good use of your dazzling skills."

"Jake Brennan gets to walk," Rebecca answered.

LaRoux shook his head repeatedly. "No way."

"Fine. Then you know what you need to do. Turn me over to the regular authorities and we'll do this by the book."

Her attitude clearly infuriated him. "You are not in the driving seat here, Kent. I don't know where you got that impression from."

"Maybe not. But you're going to an awful lot of trouble to see this deal go through."

He stared at her, openly resentful, and then answered after a time. "No promises, but I'll put this to the man in charge."

"And I want the chance to say my goodbyes to Jake as well. That's another precondition."

In the event, Rebecca got what she asked for and the two of them were allowed five minutes alone in the interview room. Jake looked raggedy, skeletal, spooked. And it was all Rebecca could do not to cry at this spectacle. "Looks like I'm off back home," he whispered softly. "They're having me repatriated. Not the worst outcome by a long stretch. I guess you're the one who's footing the bill?"

"It's alright. I'll be fine. They've obviously got big plans for me here."

Jake pulled her close to him, planted a kiss on her cheek. Then whispered in her ear. "The Old Brennan Place. Ballinamore. That's where I'll be should you ever need me."

The Old Brennan Place. She had googled it several times but was not sorry to see it turn up no results whatsoever. Better that it could only be located in person, on the ground. Jake had already mentioned the cottage to her before, explaining how it had been owned by his family for generations.

The place where he'd always felt most at ease.

CHAPTER 34

When the shrill alarm sounded, just past six in the morning, there was no way for Zhao Min to learn what was going on. From the corridor outside, he heard a succession of frantic footsteps moving in both directions, and then the sound of doors being flung open and slammed shut.

Ten minutes later, three soldiers entered his own room, led by Staff Sergeant Purdy, the man in overall charge of the main barracks. Zhao had always appreciated, and expected, the respect shown to him by the staff at PROPS, and he was glad to discover that, even under these circumstances, Purdy thought to apologise first of all. "Sorry Zhao, we need to conduct a full search of your quarters."

"No. That's fine. Please, do what you need to do."

The search proved exhaustive and the men saw fit to take all of his things apart, including Zhao's music system and personal laptop. Unlike his fellow students, Zhao Min had always retained the right to choose his possessions freely and none of the recent restrictions had applied to himself. His was still a voluntary residency and he was entitled to walk away at any time.

"May I ask what's going on?" Zhao asked.

"Sorry Zhao," Purdy answered. "Can't tell you at present. But I'm sure you'll find out soon enough."

Twenty-five minutes later, they departed from his

room. "You're going to need to stay put for the time being as well," Purdy added, before shutting the door behind him.

Zhao's room remained closed off for the next five hours, although he'd thought better of calling for any assistance or kicking up a fuss. It was clear from these measures that a serious crisis was in full swing.

It was not until midday that his door opened again and another guard escorted Zhao Min out. Together they crossed over to the main complex, but their destination was neither the lecture hall, nor the Colonel's office, as Zhao had first supposed. Instead he'd been led back through the end corridor and ushered directly into The Operations Room. Invited to take a seat at the central desk. Then the guard had withdrawn and there Zhao sat, completely unattended. A couple of moments later, the huge screen at the front of the room transmitted an image, filling up with the head and shoulders of Charles Graves. It was a shock to Zhao Min to find himself live all of a sudden with the Head of Cyber Command.

"Zhao Min."

"sir."

"You know nothing of this unfolding crisis?"

"No sir. Not as yet."

"Rebecca Kent has escaped from PROPS, aided and abetted by Professor Radan."

"I see."

"As you'd imagine, we're doing everything within our power to bring this situation back under control and I would like for you to play an integral role in these efforts."

"Of course, sir. Anything I can do to help."

"I'm placing you in temporary charge of operational matters at PROPS. I'm also sending you a number of analysts from DC to help out and provide some extra manpower. These are signs, in case you needed any, that you enjoy my complete confidence."

"Thank you, sir. That means a great deal to me."

"Time for you to step out of the shadows, Zhao. Are you ready?"

"Yes sir, I am."

"I know you're a fast learner and so I expect that what little Radan had to teach you, you've already absorbed?"

"I'm of that opinion, yes. I am totally confident in my own abilities."

"Good. On the table next to you, you'll find an up to the minute briefing on this entire situation, comprising everything we know to date. Also you'll find a wallet to one side of it, containing those security passes you'll need to access PROPS in full. From now on, I want you stationed in this room, calling the shots, starting this very minute."

"I'm on it, sir. You have my word. I will do my very best."

Graves gave a final curt nod and then the screen went blank. Zhao Min picked the wallet up and looked inside at the array of security passes. He basically had the freedom of PROPS in the palm of his hand and it caused his face to break out in a wide, self-congratulatory smile.

*

Chuck White was lying back against his bed, immersed in a daydream, when the visitor entered at noon. He looked across casually at this new arrival, although it did cause him to raise one eyebrow when the man's identity became clear. It was Zhao Min who'd entered his quarters. Furthermore, there was nobody else escorting him. This curious development caused Chuck to sit up.

"Thought you'd vetoed all social contact between me and you."

"I need you to come with me, White."

"Where we going?"

"To the Operations Room."

Chuck stayed put, showed no sign of doing as he was told. "And Rebecca?"

"Rebecca is no longer on this site. One of our immediate tasks will be to track her down."

"Oh it will, will it?"

"Yes. Unless you want me to tell Graves that your friendship with Kent and Wylde makes you unfit for this task. But I don't think this would be the best outcome you could hope for. I suggest we put all our hostility to one side. There is no time for that now."

Chuck appeared to think this over. "So they're letting us loose inside the engine room?"

"Yes. That's where we'll be based from now on. And Graves is sending over some assistance as well. Analysts from the Pentagon."

"But you get to keep operational control?"

"That is my understanding, yes. For the time being."

Chuck sprang to his feet, stretched out his limbs, and let out a yawn. "Don't be so bashful, son. Congratulations, you just made the big time. Guess this makes you the boss man, Zhao."

CHAPTER 35

It was nearly 2pm when the taxi pulled to a stop on the edge of that short high street running through the village of Ballinamore. The driver pulled over to the side of the road, wound down his window, and asked directions from a man in his sixties who was happening by, dressed in a brown plaid shirt, walking a Jack Russell on a long lead. "Would you happen to know where The Old Brennan place is?"

The dog walker considered the question for some time. "And who, might I ask, wants to know?"

"I do." Rebecca leaned forward and spoke up from the back of the car. The man leaned forwards himself, stuck his head through the car window, and peered in at Rebecca. "So it's our young hermit that you're wanting?"

"Yes. That's right."

He nodded. "I see."

"I'd go so far as to vouch for her character," said the driver. "She's seems like a good girl."

"Is that so?"

"In my humble opinion."

"And you're a Dublin man yourself?"

"That I am."

The dog walker nodded again, weighing up everything. Then, after a long pause, he told the driver exactly which directions to take.

As they passed through the town and started climbing the far road, in the direction of the Sliabh an Iariann mountains, Rebecca felt like shedding a tear for this confirmation – knowing herself, finally, to be on the right track.

They travelled some five miles, heading upwards into a bleak, beautiful landscape. On their left, after a hairpin bend, they passed by a long dilapidated outhouse, its walls in a state of ruin. "That'll be the old Creeley farm your man mentioned," the driver said. Rebecca admired his certainty. Another half a mile and he slowed the Astra, then pulled it to a stop by a tiny stone bridge running over a brook. Beyond it lay a small pathway, barely visible, where the grass had been trampled down. It rose up through a clump of Norwegian spruces and then disappeared from sight. The taxi driver gestured at this walkway with a nod. "It's up there, as I understand it. About a mile or so on foot…You want me to wait for you here, just in case?"

"No. Thanks. I'll take my chances."

"As you please. The best of luck to you."

"Thanks again."

It was only as she stepped out of the car that Rebecca began to feel nervous, and this nervousness overpowered her very recent sense of relief. The grass beneath her feet was still wet with the morning dew, darkening her trainers, and the footpath was flanked with woodland on either side. Rebecca tried staring between these trunks at the dim terrain beyond it, but her view of it was swallowed up by a deep forest gloom.

After a fifteen minute walk, Rebecca turned a final bend in the path and it made her heart leap to see the cottage straight ahead of her, smoke rising from its chimney, and it was all she could do to stop from breaking into a run. The dwelling was set down at the centre of a large yard, among a scattering of outbuildings, and must have dated from centuries ago. It had an old tin roof, sloping downwards, and the walls of the place, once whitewashed, were now discoloured and streaked with green.

Rebecca stopped five yards shy of the wooden door set in its front. "Jake," she called out.

There was no answer forthcoming and so she raised her voice again. In response there was a slight movement at the window. The flutter of a curtain. A shadow lurking behind it. Then, just as she was on the verge of making for the door, to give it a bold knock, the entrance swung slowly open and outwards and there Jake Brennan was.

She had expected a hermit's beard, but instead he was freshly shaved, which only made her friend's gauntness all the more striking. His thick black hair, in contrast, was tangled and unruly like an abandoned nest. He'd put on no weight since she'd last seen him and nor did he look any less haunted either. Worst of all, there was genuine suspicion in his eyes aimed purely at herself, and this pierced Rebecca to the core.

"Rebecca…" Jake gave her a curt nod. The look on his face remained guarded, as if he was determined to keep their old familiarity at bay.

"Seemed like the right moment to drop by," she said.

He nodded, looked down at her bags. "No laptops or mobiles in there?"

"I have a laptop Jake, yes."

"Then you need to destroy it immediately or else I'm going to have to ask you to leave."

"Can't do that, Jake. Somebody's life is at stake, and there's no other way to save them except remaining online."

He pulled a grimace, as if suffering from toothache. "Who's life?"

"Actually, make that two lives, and mine is one of them."

He rubbed the palm of his right hand over the back of his head again and again. Doing himself violence. "Jesus, Rebecca. Was there nothing for it but to travel all this way and put me on the spot?"

"You owe me, Jake. Don't forget that. That's why I'm here. Your kind offer held good for always, as I understood it. Least that's what you led me to believe."

"That much is true and I'm not pretending otherwise. I as good as owe you my life."

Rebecca saw no need to add anything more to this fact. She simply stood there.

"Then you can position yourself over by the woodshed there, if you want to conduct your business," Jake said.

"The woodshed…"

"Yes. I will not have that thing switched on inside my home."

"OK, Jake. That's fine."

"And I'll ask that you stay here no longer than is strictly necessary."

"That's not my intention."

He nodded again. "OK." Then he pushed himself back against the front door, to make room for his guest to enter. "You'd better come in."

"I'll come in once I'm done. I've got things to be getting on with out here"

"OK. As you will."

CHAPTER 36

Rebecca walked over to the woodshed. My new office space, she thought. Taking the laptop from its bag, she tried placing it on top of a level pile of newly cut wood and switched the computer on, praying that she could locate a GNS signal out here. Rebecca realised now that she should have stopped along the way and picked up a mobile phone with the money she had left. Some kind of back-up wireless connection. Instead it was this or nothing at all.

After thirty seconds her laptop registered the faintest of connections, showing up on the screen as one single bar, the lowest possible signal, and yet it appeared to be functioning all the same. Checking the battery gauge as well, Rebecca saw that she had a total of four hours left before it would be necessary to recharge the machine.

Now she went directly to her hidden email account and checked for messages. To Rebecca's delight, there was one waiting for her, containing exactly what she'd asked of Raymond Lowe. A string of twelve digits. Without hesitation, she dialled this number via a heavily encrypted VOIP protocol program and waited for a reply. There was no point in taking any further precautions. If Lowe was intent on setting her a trap then she was lost already. Rebecca needed his full co-operation. She had to hope that she'd already induced in him the correct amount of fear.

The connection rang out five times. Then five times more. Rebecca was not completely disheartened yet. It stood to reason that Lowe was in need of privacy, and maybe he was in the process of excusing himself, looking for the necessary seclusion. Then a voice came over the line, loud and clear. It said, "Who the hell is this?"

"Raymond Lowe?"

He hesitated. "Yes."

"I'm going to cut to the chase, Raymond. I need your help in relation to Jacob Wylde."

"Have you any idea where I am? Where Jacob Wylde is? Or how stupid your request sounds?"

"You need to access Jacob Wylde and get a computer into his cell."

"You must be crazy."

"Maybe. But that is not great news for you. It just means that I won't think twice before firing off that group email to your friends up in Ryker's Island, or else to those associates of theirs who are still at large. Telling them all about your happy reincarnation in the Seattle suburbs."

"Go to hell."

"It's not just yourself you need to worry about here, Raymond. You must know that."

"You're saying you'd think nothing about putting my family's lives at risk?"

"I'm saying that I want this done. Now. To save an innocent man's life. And if it doesn't get done then I go to town on you because I have absolutely nothing to lose."

"You're that runaway bitch, Rebecca Kent."

"Who or what I am is no concern of yours."

"Well you must be in a whole heap of trouble to be trying to lay this on me."

"Don't you worry about the trouble I'm in, Lowe.

Worry about your own sorry ass. The past coming back to haunt you. By the time you get home in three weeks time, I might have torn your world apart."

"Unless I rip your lungs out first."

"Face the facts. Recognise the certainties. And let's both of us move on…"

Lowe paused again and Rebecca took this as a good sign. It seemed that her threats were starting to carry. "You got any kind of plan of action whatsoever?" he asked.

"Let's start with you answering my original question. Can you get a laptop into Jacob Blackstone?"

"Impossible. Absolutely no way."

"I hope not, Raymond. For all of our sakes."

"For one thing, that would involve taking out the surveillance feeds and a whole bank of sensors."

"Doesn't sound impossible to me."

"This system is not some mickey mouse Windows XP bullshit. Its security features are all cutting-edge. Tailor made."

"I'm sure they are. But I'm also sure you must have an excellent understanding of the system architecture. You're an 'Executive Surveillance Technician', Raymond, so I'm guessing you'll be able to draw me a map, as well as rearranging matters yourself."

He laughed bitterly. "OK, all right, let's say we can find a way round the entire surveillance protocol. And what do I say to Wylde's personal security detail, Garcia, when he stops me and asks what I'm doing on D1?"

"Why? Does he share a room with Jacob Wylde?"

"As good as."

"Then let's make sure Garcia's presence is required elsewhere."

Lowe thought about this. "That's a tall order," he said.

"But again, not impossible."

"Maybe. Maybe not."

"And your main comms are running via what? A military satellite?"

"Yes."

"With TCP acceleration?"

"Of course."

"And what kind of spec would this laptop have? The one with Wylde's name on it."

"The kind of spec you'd expect from a government issued device at a top secret holding facility," Lowe answered.

"And can you take a charger in as well?"

"No point. There are no power sources in that cell. It's not that kind of room."

"Then what's the optimum battery life?"

"I'd say 10-12 hours."

"Then you make sure to charge that device up with all the juice you can," Rebecca said. "Oh, and I want you to include a phone in this delivery."

"Will that be all?" Raymond Lowe's breathing sounded heavy and tormented. He knew himself to be boxed into a corner with only one way out. A way he was less than convinced by. "Listen, this is only going to work by running some heavy voodoo on the whole system."

"I can do that, Raymond. We can do that. Both of us pulling together in the name of truth and justice. What could be nobler?"

"OK, let's get this over with. Where exactly do you want to start?"

CHAPTER 37

From his office up on K/12, Raymond Lowe ran a full diagnostic check on the Grey-3 Surveillance System for any tell-tale signs of what he and Rebecca Kent had just done. Thankfully, as of yet, their handiwork had not registered at all. Everything appeared to be running smoothly.

The feeds had been taken care of, and Jacob Wylde's cell was now showing yesterday's footage instead of providing any real-time coverage of events inside. A deception which would continue indefinitely on a constant loop. Also, Wylde's personal security detail, Garcia, had been summoned to the Staff Medical Ward for a psychological assessment to get him out of the way. These were performed on all personnel from time to time, with no warning given in advance, and so hopefully it would not arouse the guard's suspicion. In Garcia's absence, another Grade 1 Security Head, John Collins, had been assigned the role of standing in for him. Only Collins knew nothing about this proposed substitution. What Raymond Lowe had created, in effect, was an absence to exploit.

Lastly, they had extended the powers of Lowe's security pass, granting it universal access to the facility, as well as preventing the key from having its details logged. Nothing of his day's movements would be recorded for digital reference. From the system's point of view, it would be as though he'd kept to his standard routine.

All this Raymond Lowe had achieved over a course of four hours with a great deal of help from Rebecca Kent. She was good. Very good. Lowe hated to admit it, but under the circumstances it came as a relief to have such a talented partner in crime.

The second half of the plan was equally tricky, if not the hardest part of all. His journey in person to Jacob's Wylde's cell. Lowe leaned over his desk and brought up the schematics of the facility and looked one last time at the course he'd plotted for himself. The only possible way of reaching this goal.

The last time he'd entered a prisoner's cell was last year. To upgrade the anterior camera system. But that was nine months ago and the security protocol had changed since then. A new post had been created in the meantime for all hands-on repairs, which meant that Lowe would have no legitimate reason for being on D1. Therefore he would need to explain his presence away, should anybody care to ask.

There were only three manned checkpoints along the route which Lowe had chosen for himself. At the first two, he could tell them that he was bound for the Comms Hub down on C/7. The third and final barrier was the most difficult to penetrate. But there was no other way for him to access D1 without passing this threshold, and by that point, his destination would be absolutely clear to the security personnel stationed there.

Lowe checked his terminal to see who was on duty. Thomas Franklin. It could have been a whole lot worse. This was a man he often socialised with outside of work hours. Ten nights ago, Franklin had taken 600 dollars off him at a poker game conducted on the quiet. In hindsight, this now seemed like a positive thing, and

Lowe had never been so happy to have lost money in his life.

Now Lowe lifted the laptop from his table and placed it into the bag by his side. Zipped the bag up. He took a deep breath and blew it out with an air of resignation. Then he departed the room.

At the end of the corridor, the security guard for the whole technical floor looked up without batting an eyelid. Here it was enough for Lowe to lift up his bag and say, "Comms Hub." before turning to face the lift entrance.

He inserted his security key into the control panel to bring up an elevator. It arrived swiftly and he used the key again inside of it and rode it down to C/2. At the entrance to this floor, Lowe was inspected by another guard, stationed behind perspex, and obliged to explain himself. Lowe performed the same little mime as before, lifting up his laptop bag as if it made everything perfectly clear. Then he gave the same destination. Comms Hub. And again the guard responded by unlocking the double doors for Lowe to pass through.

The corridor on the other side was long, wide, deserted. Lowe walked a total of forty metres, praying no-one else would enter this passage, and stopped by the nearest transit point. He looked around nervously, applied his key card to the panel, and hailed another elevator. It arrived twenty seconds later and he stepped swiftly inside. Then the carriage shot upwards and in no time at all he found himself deposited on D1.

Out in the hallway, twenty metres up ahead, Lowe could see the final checkpoint in his way, and he tried walking towards it with all the confidence he could muster. Thomas Franklin, up in his security booth, watched Lowe's passage with a smile. "Hey. Look who it is. Cool Hand Luke."

"Very funny, Franklin," Lowe answered, stopping in

front of the reinforced metal doors. "You gonna give me a chance to win that money back some time soon?"

"Is that what you think's going to happen?"

"Certainly do."

"A fool and his money. It's a beautiful combination. So what brings you to down to D/1?"

Lowe lifted up his bag for a third time. "A maintenance issue with the anterior surveillance feeds."

"Don't you have minions for that kind of thing? Thought you were moving up in the world."

"Cameras were updated as of last week. Now they're supposed to be running new software. An XQB platform. Thing is, nobody else but me in this place is qualified to make this amendment on-site." He turned up his eyes, as if this was not the first time that such a problem had occurred.

"New security protocols without the personnel to oversee them. Yeh, that sounds about right."

"Tell me about it," Lowe answered.

Franklin nodded agreeably and opened the doors to D1.

Lowe walked the last half kilometre without meeting any further challenge and came to a stop outside of D1/Y. He punched in the day's security code, acquired earlier from the operating system, and with this the cell door clicked open.

He stepped inside, shut the door behind him. There was Jacob Wylde lying on his bunk, hiding his face behind the crook of his elbow, shielding his eyes from the room's harsh light. When Wylde took this elbow away, and stared over at his visitor, Lowe thought that the young Englishman appeared both dazed and defeated. "Time to wake the hell up and prove you've been framed," Lowe said.

It was a startling introduction and had an immediate

effect on Jacob. He propped himself up on his elbows. "What do you mean?"

Lowe went into his bag and pulled the laptop out and placed it down on the small table. "I understand you know how to use one of these."

Instinctively, Jacob looked up at the cameras in his room.

"They're showing yesterday's feed on a loop. Nobody can see in here. Only thing you need to worry about in the short term is Garcia paying you an unannounced visit."

"Where is he now?"

"I sent him off to get his mental health seen to, but it's not impossible that he might smell a rat. You have been warned," Lowe said. "Oh, and here's your back-up as well." And with this, he removed a mobile device from his trouser pocket and placed this on the table also.

Jacob sprang up off the bed, walked over to the table, stood by the laptop as if he could hardly bring himself to touch it. "I don't know how to thank you," he said.

"Don't thank me at all, Wylde. If your bitch of a girlfriend – if that's what she is – hadn't blackmailed me, I wouldn't be here now. It was this or else risk my family's life."

Jacob nodded, couldn't help but smile.

"I just hope you're every bit as good as she says you are. Otherwise we're both completely screwed."

Jacob felt a surge of energy in line with this brand new hope. Adrenalin firing round his system. "I know what I need to do," he said.

"Kent says you're not working for the Chinese."

"That's right."

"Well you'd better get on with proving that to be true. For everyone's sakes."

"I intend to. Thanks."

"Like I said. Spare me the gratitude."

"All right."

Lowe looked at Jacob closely, as if wanting to believe in him. Then he shook his head, turned his back, and departed the cell; locking it once more from the outside.

"Nice vote of confidence there," Jacob muttered to himself.

Then he powered the computer up.

CHAPTER 38

The laptop Raymond Lowe had smuggled into the cell was running a hot-wired version of Linux. Jacob checked on its connectivity as well and saw that his link-up to the net was via a geostationary military satellite called PAK-TEL. The specs on the laptop were fit for use, including 6 core Intel Xeon processors and 24GB of DDR3. He only had to hope the battery on the machine would provide him with time enough to clear his name. Now Jacob clicked the power icon in the left hand corner of the screen. It stated he had 11 hours and 32 minutes to play with, although chances were the clock would run down quicker given the multitasking he had in mind.

Looking at those programmes icons on the screen, one of them stood out above all others.

VPN – Rebecca Kent.

Jacob clicked it open at once and typed in her name.

Rebecca???

There was an agonising wait of twenty seconds and then a message appeared:

– I'm here, but I've only got 5 mins of battery time left. Need 2 recharge.

– Where r you?

– Country Leitrim. The wilds of Ireland.

– How the hell did u manage to pull that off?

– Native cunning, dumb luck, Professor Radan. So what next?

– This has to be an inside job. Someone back at PROPS must have stitched me up. We need to track them down.

– There's a trapdoor already in place to access the system. Radan put it there. He's also put all his own software onto my computer. So far it's saved me a whole bunch of time and trouble. I'm going to send it 2 u now.

– Ok. You had a chance 2 explore PROPS in depth?

– No. Not yet.

– Well I'm going to take a look. Chase up evidence. Maybe u can target the key suspects, examine them as well?

– We don't have long. You think this is the best way forward?

– If you have any better ideas, I'm open to them...

– Ok. I'll give it a shot. Got to go now and recharge this machine.

– Ok, let me know when you're back online.

– Will do.

– I miss u.

– I know. X

With Rebecca signed off, Jacob waited for Professor Radan's suite of software to finish downloading. Then he opened it up, installed the package, and spent the best part of ten minutes figuring out how best to apply it in these extreme circumstances.

To do what needed doing.

Jacob was eager to access the PROPS servers immediately, but it occurred to him he needed to strengthen his hand first and take out a little insurance in case the alarm bells went off too soon. To this end, he put plans in place to evacuate PAK-TEL if necessary, and piggyback onto another geostationary satellite.

Then he accessed the detention facility via a trapdoor designed by Raymond Lowe, and went into its operating system to make a series of adjustments. As the last of these came into effect, Jacob looked back at the clock. The whole business had taken him 45 minutes. He knew he could not allocate the task any more of his precious resources and had to hope his efforts would work in the event. It was now time to move on and pursue his enemy.

Using Radan's trapdoor, Jacob entered the PROPS servers. It did not take him long to discover what he was looking for. The document was now circulating to everybody at the facility with a high-ranking security clearance.

The Case Against Jacob Wylde: A Preliminary Report.

Compiled by a senior CIA data analyst by the name of Thomas O'Hara, Jacob brought up its table of contents, studied the options, and decided to start at the end with its Summary Conclusion.

In short, Wylde discovered a method for disabling the keystroke protocol at PROPS. This allowed him to avoid all proper surveillance and create a dummy-front which gave the appearance of routine laptop usage. With the time and freedom created by this clandestine procedure, he was then able to greatly expand the laptop's connectivity and elude all imposed controls. In this way contact with the Chinese military intelligence was duly established. The programming involved in this feat was of a highly sophisticated nature and it was only after fifteen straight hours of forensic examination that I was able to detect the true nature of Wylde's activity. For further clarification, please refer to the relevant data logs.

Jacob clicked on this link and scrolled down the page, reading the code attributed to himself. It was obvious that whoever lay behind this deceit was a real professional, and he almost found himself admiring this slippery customer even as he strove to pin down the person's identity. The programming was elegant and vaguely familiar to him, leaving Jacob with the nagging sense that he'd seen its like before.

Now Jacob turned to the alleged correspondence between himself and the Chinese military. Starting with his opening offer to be of service to them. In this message, he had appeared to pledge all available help in accessing Cyber Command's servers, as a token of his "sincerity". Longer term, he'd promised to place his powers at their complete disposal "for the rest of my living days" on the condition that they agreed to spring him from the complex.

If you can get me out of here then you have already seen what I can do.

In reply, the Chinese had guaranteed to secure Jacob's release from PROPS within the next twelve months. In the meantime, to show their good faith, a series of large payments had been channelled into an unnumbered Swiss bank account.

So it went on and on. A disastrous tissue of lies.

Jacob' point of contact with the Chinese had been traced back to a secure server based in Macau, belonging to a casino called The New Imperial, long believed to be a front for Chinese intelligence. Now that same rumour appeared to have been confirmed, and at the bottom of the relevant paragraph, he read the following:

More information on The New Imperial's operating system can be found here.

Jacob clicked on the link but nothing happened, even though he saw the power light on his computer blinking furiously and could hear its processor working overtime. As he tried to bring up a diagnostic overview to see what had caused this sudden spike in use, all the PROPS windows closed and Jacob realised he'd been kicked out of the system altogether. Suddenly, before he could react further, the screen on his laptop went blank. Then, from the depths of this blackness, a tiny digital animation appeared. At the same time, old guitar music started up on his computer's speakers.

As this animated figure moved towards the foreground and grew in size, Jacob could see that it was a jester dressed in full traditional costume, moving in time to the music. Then, as the character came nearer still, Jacob saw that a real human face had been grafted onto the digital image, its features showing beneath the jester's hat.

It bore the face of Chuck White.

The accompanying song also grew louder, ending with the chuckle of its lead singer:

Heh-heh-heh-heh...Wipeout!

Now text began to appear at the bottom of the screen, as if spray-painted there by an aerosol can:

Viva Bungalow Bill! Taking Out Little Jacob Wylde With A Technical K.O!!!!!

At this, the figure swivelled both hands around and gave him the finger twice. Watching the spectacle unfold, Jacob realised that this was who the programming had first reminded him of. All that code linking him mistakenly with the Chinese. In hindsight, he recognised the same trademark flourishes as belonging to his classmate.

So his real enemy was Chuck White.

As Jacob considered his options, the display changed again and the Command Line Interface came into view. At the same time, alien text started raining down the screen, bombarding his operating system with attack scripts. Chuck had somehow avoided the Intrusion

Detection software and attached himself to those stealth ports Jacob had in use. Now he was was busy injecting ruinous code onto the laptop.

Quickly, Jacob brought up one of Radan's tools, RePEL, and ran the program in an effort to block all traffic from Chuck's IP address and stem the ongoing carnage. At the same he started a denial of service attack, hitting back with a succession of TCP SYN floods. "Come on, Come on," he muttered, but his efforts proved useless and the infection continued to rage. There was no option left except to surrender further ground to the malware and try to protect the machine's inner core. The vital kernel of programming. To this end, Jacob started hammering out code on the keyboard to try and ringfence this hub.

Twenty minutes roared by, and by the time Jacob could put a stop to the attack, he had no idea what was left for him to work with. His laptop was now sluggish as hell and it took five minutes to even bring up a systems log. To add to his misery, Jacob saw that a mere 17% of the laptop's operating capacity still remained in place. The list of disk failures and corrupted drivers was seemingly endless, although thankfully the computers' superblock information had been preserved and he would therefore be able to recreate the array.

In the meantime, there was still the hand-held device Lowe had brought in. The latest Samsung Galaxy. But it simply didn't have the firepower he needed right now.

It took Jacob a further five minutes to start-up SaLVE, Radan's Rebuild program for Linux. The best chance he had of piecing together the hard drive and making deep structural repairs. And while the program slowly wheeled into action, he had little choice but to try and think out his next move in light of this devastating realisation.

The betrayal of a friend.

Had this betrayal been under way from the moment that they'd first met, he wondered. Was all that initial warmth no more than a cover behind which Chuck's malice had continued to grow? And why finger Jacob for this crime? Chuck, by his own admission, was all about the Benjamins. Was this the reason then? Financial reward?

At least White had dared announce himself as a foe. It was not an obvious sign of weakness – more an act of bravado – but maybe this amounted to the same thing. Perhaps Chuck now expected Jacob to rise to the bait and engage in a duel, but he knew that would only be a waste of time. Exactly what Chuck wanted. In that way he might tangle with Jacob for hours on end and run down the last of the clock.

No. Jacob needed to somehow re-route his escape plan. Find another way. Think outside the box. There had to be an alternative.

He strained his mind, trying to process every single thing that had happened since the moment Wilkins first entered his bedroom back in Liverpool and brought an end to his regular life. Sifting through these months, Jacob returned to the flight which had taken him to North Carolina and zoned back in on his conversation with Charles Graves; the way in which Graves had denied the existence of Quantica.

Even at the time, it had struck Jacob that Graves was trying too hard to throw him off the scent. Now, once again, he considered that fabled Pentagon server and holy grail of hackers worldwide. As things stood, Jacob realised he was left with little option except to stake everything on his fierce hunch and prove it correct. Maybe, just maybe, with Radan's suite of software in play, and his own powers at their current height, Jacob could locate Quantica and somehow gain entry to it. Come away with that mother lode of data which had obsessed him for months on end. If so, he could stop the clock from ticking. Buy himself time. Time enough to unmask Chuck White.

CHAPTER 39

Zhao Min and Chuck White looked up from their desk inside the Operations Room as the door to it opened. Five men in suits filed in, staring around them at the hardware on display.

"Washington's finest," said Chuck.

Zhao stood up and welcomed his colleagues sombrely. "Good afternoon. You'll see that terminals have been made available for you here. I would ask that you sit down and familiarise yourselves with our set-up as quickly as possible. We have no time to waste…" As the analysts followed Zhao's lead, he continued: "I understand two of you specialise in facial recognition, so I want you to start searching every database worldwide, no matter how obscure, for a recent match with Rebecca Kent. Everyone else, I need you to work through Professor Radan's PROPS directories. One of you to flag up any packets of data which might betray Kent's whereabouts. The other two to see if there's anything in there which might compromise our own security. It's not impossible that there are a few advanced rootkits allowing ready access to this facility, if not the whole of Cyber Command. Obviously we need to rip these out. Any questions?…No?…OK. Let's go to it. If we all pull together I'm confident that we can turn this situation around."

"Shit," said Chuck, under his breath but still loud

enough to be heard "This must be like your ultimate wet dream to the power of ten."

Zhao span round in response. "If you've got nothing useful to say, White, then I suggest you say nothing. There is no longer any audience here for your amusing remarks, in case you hadn't noticed, and if you continue with this endless stream of sarcasm then I will have you expelled from this room. Considering where your mind is at right now, I don't know that it would represent a huge loss."

At this, Chuck took hold of his monitor and moved it around for Zhao to see the bustle of activity taking place on the screen."Just take a look at that and try telling me that I'm not pulling my weight like a good soldier. You have my backing, 100%."

As Zhao stared back at Chuck, less than convinced, the phone next to his terminal sounded and he snatched it up at the first ring. "Hello. This is Zhao Min…" It was clear from his face that the news was significant and positive. After a minute, he placed the phone back down. "She's in Ireland," Zhao declared. "We now have a positive ID from customs official at both ends. Kent must have somehow got her hands on a passport which negated all existing border controls."

"With a little help from Radan," Chuck commented.

"Quite possibly," Zhao said.

"And you know where exactly in the country she's headed?" Chuck asked.

"Not yet. But it shouldn't be long in coming, that information. Not if we train our efforts in the right direction. This narrows the search down to manageable parameters. I want all efforts focused on Ireland as of now. Satellite, police liaison, CCT. Everything."

For the next twenty minutes, the room was quiet except for the furious typing of all seven men. Many of them scenting a chance to make a name for themselves. The first person to speak again was Chuck White. "Hello…." He was looking at his screen, intrigued by what he saw there.

Zhao Min got up from his seat for a better look "What is it? You've got a position on Kent?"

"Nope. At least I don't think so. But I've got me an intruder here, tippy-toeing around the PROPS servers. Looks like a real live wire."

"Where is it originating from, the signal?"

"Impossible to say at present, but they're going for broke."

"You're on top of this?"

"Don't worry. Give me a minute and I'll pin the signal down."

Chuck leaned forwards, inches from his screen, and appeared to run an advanced back-trace on the intruder. Another three minutes and the program returned a single IP address. "Ok. I think I've got a location."

"Where is it? Ireland?" Zhao asked.

"No. Not Ireland. A tiny dot, somewhere in the South Atlantic. Close to Antarctica." Chuck turned around in his chair and looked directly at Zhao. "Not trying to speak out of turn here – but mightn't that be Jacob's current residence?"

Zhao looked back at Chuck, and then towards that analyst sat to his right. "Get me Graves on the phone," he said.

CHAPTER 40

The high-pitched alarm sounded throughout the whole of Grey-3 for a total of ten seconds, with ear-splitting intensity, and then it stopped dead. Exactly as Jacob Wylde had instructed it to do. Coming less than twenty minutes after Chuck's venomous attack, it was only what he'd expected to hear.

The contest had now moved on.

Checking the laptop, Jacob saw that its operational capacity was now back up to 61%. After a moment's hesitation, he decided to make use of these limited resources by running a check on Grey-3's operating system: to confirm that it was responding to his own commands. Earlier he had rerouted the alarm system to produce very different results to those expected by the jail's personnel. Now Jacob checked on the underlying schematics of the facility and saw that red X's were being displayed at every juncture throughout the building, confirming that a complete lockdown had taken hold.

Every room, floor, elevator, all of them were barred to Grey-3's staff. Confining them to whichever quarters they happened to find themselves in. On top of this – as he now verified – Jacob had disabled the digital sphere as well, with every single computer terminal taken out of use, leaving himself as the only administrator still at large, directing proceedings throughout the facility. He'd even jammed their mobile devices.

As well as safeguarding his independence, Jacob had opened up another front. If the boys back at PROPS wanted to try their hands at overturning this code, then all the better. It would cost them no small effort and take up a good deal of time. Time in which Jacob could busy himself with his gameplan.

Going for broke.

Now he began to operate the satellite dish fixed to the roof of Grey-3, moving it around to find an alternative connection as his PAK-TEL signal had been compromised. There were a number of choices, but Jacob opted for a an illicit link-up with a Low Earth Orbit platform, Saturnalia, normally used to broadcast television to South America. After establishing this fresh connection, Jacob brought up the VPN and saw that Rebecca was still away from it. Still, he left a message for her there.

It's Chuck White. Looks like he might be in league with the Chinese military. I haven't time to explain further. I've got one idea left as to what I can do. This will all be decided one way or the other in the next couple of hours. In the meantime, please lie low and stay safe.

J.

xxx

Again Jacob monitored the status of the laptop and saw that its systems integrity was back up to 68%. That would have to do for now. He didn't have time to wait for it to reach its optimal performance. Jacob also looked at the Battery Meter and saw that it had dropped to 8 hours and 21 minutes. The Repair program on its own had been making great inroads into the available power supply. And his consumption was about to get a whole lot heavier, given the rate of activity Jacob was about to pursue – pushing this machine to the max.

He sat up straight, cracked every knuckle, readied himself for the challenge.

Raise his game or else die.

Chapter 41

When Rebecca entered the cottage, Jake was nowhere to be seen inside its front room. She set down her rucksack and computer bag against the side of a battered armchair and called out his name, but heard nothing in reply. The space was cluttered, stale, comprising a lounge, small dining area, rough and ready kitchenette. The grimy net curtains were keeping out the last of the daylight and every window was closed firmly.

Rebecca called Jake's name again and stepped carefully towards that half open door beyond the corner sink. She peered inside and saw a small empty bathroom. Another door, off to her right, was pulled to and Rebecca thought better of opening it. Maybe Jake was sleeping in there or simply keeping his distance, although just as likely he'd left the cottage behind without her noticing. Either by way of a back door or even by passing right in front of Rebecca as she'd stood there in the woodshed, focused on the tasks at hand.

There was not much to see in that front room, little of any personal value. A makeshift bookshelf had been knocked up over the neglected fireplace, but it contained no books on programming or computer sciences as would once have been the case. Not even any of Jake's favourite authors were on display. No Gibson, Sterling, or Phillip K.Dick. In their place stood guides to edible mushrooms, bushcraft, and earth skills.

Rebecca had no desire to explore the cottage beyond these few items. No need either. Everything important that was to be known about Jake, and what the last two years had done to him, was there to see in the man himself.

Realising this was a good opportunity to recharge the laptop, Rebecca found a socket down behind the two-person sofa, plugged in the lead, and affixed it to the computer. She checked to see if it was working and was much relieved to watch the green power light come on. It wouldn't have been a huge surprise if Jake had done away with electricity altogether and fallen back on candlelight, but thankfully this was not so.

Rebecca stood up now and flicked on the light switch to do away with the gathering gloom. As she could feel herself tiring again, she went looking for something to combat this sensation. No coffee there on the kitchen sideboard, but she spotted a box of teabags and placed two of these inside a large mug while checking the nearby kettle for water. As it was hall full, she switched the dented kettle on and then went and sat down at the small dining table on the one wooden chair.

The time was 7.14pm according to the clock on the wall. 3.14 pm in North Carolina. 6.14pm in the South Atlantic. Rebecca had to hope against hope that Jacob could work a miracle in the allotted time. Maybe he'd already fingered the culprit and put a stop to this terrible mess. Although, just as likely, he'd been frustrated completely and his efforts had come to nothing.

As the water began to boil, she got up to pour it into her mug. Then the front door opened from outside and Jake entered. He was wearing a battered old hunting jacket. Resting against one shoulder, a 16 gauge shotgun. Slung across the other one, a brace of dead rabbits. Rebecca froze instinctively, fearing some wild accusation, as if she might be thought of as taking liberties in making herself a mug of tea. But Jake smiled at her instead. It was not the great big grin of old, but nonetheless it represented the first warm gesture she'd received from him since arriving.

"You got enough hot water on the go for another brew?" he asked.

"Sure have."

Jake placed the game on the table and stood by the single rackety chair. "Thought I'd cook us a stew this evening."

"I don't have time, Jake."

"You need to eat Rebecca. If not this, then something. At least let me make you a sandwich. I've got some fresh cheese in the fridge."

"Ok. A sandwich is good."

As Rebecca made the drinks, Jake came over and prepared the snack for her. "Listen," he said. "I'm sorry about that frosty welcome before. It was a shock to the system seeing you standing there like that and I know I didn't respond in the best way."

"That's all right. I'm sorry myself for turning up out of the blue. Only I really had no other options."

"So you're on the run?"

"That's something of an understatement."

Jake nodded. "There's an old camper van, a mile up the trail. I thought to leave some bedding inside there this afternoon and make it habitable. It's running on an old diesel generator. So if you're OK spending the night in there then you can do all the computing you like. It also means you might have yourself a small head start once the cavalry shows up."

"No-one knows I'm here, Jake."

He smiled sceptically. "You always were more optimistic than me."

"I'll leave Leitrim tonight if that's what you think."

He shook his head forcefully. "No. I won't hear of it. I do still care for you a lot, Becca, in my own curious way, and I'm glad for the chance to show it."

"Jake..." She took hold of his hand. He allowed her to do so and gave it a short squeeze in return. "I'll be gone by tomorrow. I promise. It will all be over by then, one way or another. As for now, I know there's so much for us to catch up on, but I'm going to head to the camper. I really don't have any time to waste."

Jake nodded. "I understand." He moved over to an old dresser in one corner of the room and opened up a drawer full of odds and ends. There he located a small Maglite torch, switched it on and off. ""Here. You'll need this as well. It's less than a mile, the old camper. Just follow the path beyond the woodshed." Then he went over to the kitchen sideboard and came back with her sandwich in his other hand, already wrapped in foil. "One cheese sandwich to go," Jake said.

Rebecca came forward and hugged him tight. "Thanks Jake. For all of your help. I mean it."

"You're welcome, Becca."

She then went over to her things, unplugged the laptop, and put it in her bag along with the lead. "Well, I'll say goodnight then."

"Night, night." Jake's face looked shrunken, weary, but no longer upset.

Torch in hand, she left by the front door and went out into the Leitrim evening, in the direction of the camper van. It was time to find out if there was any hope left.

CHAPTER 42

When Zhao Min reached Graves on the phone, he was told by his superior to leave the Operations Room at once and continue along the corridor until he'd reached the Secure Conferencing Area.

By the time Zhao had accessed this other room, the main screen was already switched on inside of it and he was confronted with three remote figures all gathered in one place, only waiting for his arrival. They were sat around an oval table inside The Special Situations Room, deep inside the Pentagon itself. This inner circle consisted of Head of Cyber Command, Charles Graves; a five-star General, William Barnes; and Secretary of Defence, Robert Purdy.

"Zhao," Graves nodded.

"Mr Graves, Secretary of Defence Purdy, General Barnes."

"How are your efforts progressing to regain control of Grey-3?" The Secretary of Defence asked.

"These efforts are ongoing, sir. Progress is being made. And I remain hopeful that overall control of the facility can be regained shortly," Zhao answered.

"Would you care to give us an estimated time frame for this?" asked General Barnes.

Zhao paused. "I am certainly confident we can make a breakthrough soon."

"Confident is not going to cut it at this point,"

General Barnes hit back. "Can you, or can you not, provide the necessary guarantees that this will be over within the next hour?"

"No sir, I cannot."

"So there is no way for you to shut Wylde down any time soon?"

Zhao paused, coughed into his fist, then shook his head. "No sir, I cannot be certain of this."

"Wylde is an exceptional talent," Graves added.

"An exceptional security threat," the General replied. "As we can now see."

"Have efforts not been made to close down his satellite comms?"asked Purdy.

"Yes," Zhao answered, "but it's clear that he's already vacated PAK-TEL and it's proving very difficult to trace his current whereabouts. He could, in theory, piggyback onto any other satellite currently in orbit."

" I think it's fair to say, there's no knowing what he's capable of right now," Graves added.

"And what about Kent?" asked the Secretary of Defence.

"Here I have better news," Zhao replied. "I can state with absolute confidence that we'll have identified her location, to the nearest kilometre, within the next half hour."

"With all due respect, Robert, Kent is no more than a sideshow here," General Barnes interjected. "The question is simple. How do we take Wylde out? I believe I'm right in thinking we have no choice but to terminate this individual at the first opportunity."

Graves nodded. "I think that's a fair assessment. Every second he is in possession of a computer, and the ability to link that computer to the outside world, means that this country must remain under serious threat. The Project Eames incident was one thing, but here you could end up with a situation whereby our most prized military secrets become a matter of public record. Either that or they end up in the hands of the Chinese."

"He could do that?" Purdy asked.

"Well, we've taken all possible preventative measures to make sure that doesn't happen. Nonetheless, he's the best at what he does. By some distance. And that makes him – and this is no exaggeration – the most dangerous individual on the planet right now. The threat level here is off the charts."

Purdy looked down at the writing pad in front of him, on which he'd been keeping detailed notes. "So what we're saying here is that we have no option but to launch a strike against our own facility. One which has so far cost in excess of eight billion pounds."

"I suspect we can limit the structural damage," Graves said. "Is that not so, General?"

"It is," Barnes replied. "In fact I'm sure we can make this hit pretty damn surgical. After all, we know exactly where the target is. Wylde's not moving from that cell. All we need to do is bring him into range and press the trigger on him."

"Collateral casualties?" Purdy asked.

Graves replied. "As things stand, we believe there are no security personnel within the vicinity of D1. The probability is that peripheral casualties will be minimal and extend to no more than a couple of inmates."

"Compared to the alternatives, I'd say that's a pretty good scenario," Barnes chipped in.

"Charles?"

"I agree with General Barnes," Graves answered. "I don't think this is something we can afford to put off."

"And our nearest operational platform?"

"That would be Chile, sir. We've got a squadron of F-16 Falcons on manoeuvres in the country. They're certainly equipped to get the job done."

"What would the ETA be?"

"Approximately one hour," the General informed him.

Purdy paused briefly, looked down one last time at his notepad. "OK then, lets get those planes up in the air. Once the president is done meeting with the Russian premier, we'll get him on the line to make the final call."

"Yes, sir."

Now Purdy looked away from his fellow cabinet members and addressed Zhao Min via the camera link. "Thank you for your frank assessment, Zhao. We'll be back in touch if necessary. In the meantime, keep us briefed on any significant developments."

"Of course, sir. I certainly will.

＊

As Zhao Min re-entered the operations room, Chuck swivelled round in his chair and shared the good news. "I've got the final co-ordinates here for Rebecca."

"Good. Where is she?"

"The county of Leitrim. Just outside a town called Ballinamore."

Zhao picked up his phone."I'll pass this on immediately."

"Is there no way we can get them to go easy on her?" Chuck asked.

"That's out of our hands, White. Kent has made her own choices. Now she must live with them."

"It's more her dying that concerns me."

"Well I'm sure they would much prefer to question her, if it comes to that."

"You're probably right. Listen, I need a power snooze. Just twenty minutes. I'm totally bushed. Is that OK?"

Zhao looked at Chuck closely, then nodded. "Of course. I must confess you deserve it, White. Your efforts so far have been admirable and I will make sure that Graves hears of this."

"That's mighty kind of you, partner."

Zhao went into his trouser pocket and took out the full set of security cards. He separated one pass from the others and then offered this to Chuck. "There's a sleeping bay, three doors down. This will permit you access to it. You can rest in there."

"Will do."

Chapter 43

After walking for ten minutes, Rebecca turned a sharp bend in the woodland path. She heard the cawing of crows up on her left and then watched a murder of them clearing the tree tops, climbing skywards against the last of the evening light. There ahead of her was an old Volkswagen camper van standing on cinder blocks, its original beige paintwork turned a sickly green with age, neglect, bad weather. Rebecca approached the crippled vehicle and tried the handle on the side door. It swung open freely and she climbed up inside, switching on the Maglite to illuminate this space.

The inside of the van looked to be an improvement on its exterior, and although it smelt old and decrepit, Jake had done more than simply bring bedding in. He'd also cleaned the camper out as well and aired it for a time. Also, Rebecca could hear the hum of the generator at work, underneath the chassis, already providing power. For that reason, she tried a switch on the side panel and the room lit up at once. There was a single cot at the far end. Nearer to the door, a small low table set into the floor with cushioned benches either side of it. Rebecca sat herself down on the nearest of these, leaned back against its flimsy tartan padding, and took the Dell laptop from its bag. Then she switched the laptop on. Plugged in its lead.

When the machine had booted up, Rebecca opened

the VPN to see if Jacob was available to talk. There she found a message waiting for her.

It's Chuck White . Looks like he might be in league with the Chinese military. I haven't time to explain further. I've got one idea left as to what I can do. This will all be decided one way or the other in the next couple of hours. In the meantime, please lie low and stay safe.

J

xxx

It was a lot to take in. That Chuck White should be the driving force behind this treachery was not so hard to believe. Certainly she'd considered the possibility earlier. But as for Jacob's own response – it sounded very much like he'd embarked on a last ditch effort to save them both.

All or nothing. Do or die.

She typed in his name. Jacob? Tried this again, twenty seconds later. Jacob? But there was no answer and Rebecca realised he must have throw himself into the desperate task at hand. As for his advice – to lie low and stay safe – Rebecca had a serious problem with it. There had to be something she might still do to further their cause. If this would all be decided one way or the other in the next couple of hours, then there was something to be said for throwing any remaining caution to the wind.

She tried visualising in her mind the whole sorry picture, looking for some way to intervene in it. Jacob was no doubt applying his technical wizardry to the situation, so it was more the human side of things Rebecca considered now. Those existing power dynamics. Wasn't there anybody whose help they might enlist, based on this new information, who might act on the tip off?

There was only one angle of attack, as far as Rebecca could see. It was by no means certain, or even likely, but still it struck her as worth a shot. As they didn't have much of a hand left to play, there seemed little point in keeping these few cards hidden.

Rebecca entered the PROPS servers via Radan's trapdoor. This time it took longer to access than earlier, but eventually the connection was enabled, permitting her to continue along. She brought up Zhao Min's details, looking for a way to contact him, and saw that his profile had been freshly revised. Acting Head of PROPS was the title given next to his name "Well, well…" It was an encouraging development. At least if she could convince him of the truth, then he was in a strong position to intervene. It helped that their own relationship had always been cordial as far as it went. Aided by Rebecca's tendency to underplay her own abilities. This meant that Zhao Min had always seen her as the least distinct threat of them all.

She located Zhao's intranet address for PROPS. By her own reckoning, Rebecca had two and a half minutes to make herself understood before they could trace her physical location to Ballinamore. It would have to be a direct appeal based on Zhao's huge professional ambitions and his great hatred of Chuck White.

She typed in the first instant message. Zhao?

Ten seconds later, she entered his name again. Zhao?

– Who is this?

– Rebecca Kent.

….

– No stalling, Zhao. I haven't got the time.

– Go on.

– Jacob has discovered that it was Chuck White who set him up. He's working for the Chinese government.

– .And you have hard evidence of this?

– Not yet. That's going to take more time. But it was definitely him.

– Then all I can say is let me know when you have this proof to hand.

– There isn't the time for that, Zhao, and you know it. We need you to intervene directly.

– Intervene how exactly?

– By bringing this charge out into the open and putting things on hold.

– So you suggest I approach Cyber Command without a trace of evidence, basing my opinion on a fugitive's word?

– Then at least take a closer look at this yourself. This can only be good for your career, Zhao.

– If you didn't know already, I've been appointed acting head of PROPS with Graves's blessing.

– Ok. Fine. But unmask White and maybe you get to make the post your own on a permanent basis. Certainly it would be another feather in your cap. The evidence is there, Zhao, it just needs uncovering.

– I'm sorry, Rebecca, but this sounds to me like an act of desperation and nothing more. It's impossible for me to take your word on this matter.

– He's innocent, Zhao. 100%.

Now Rebecca looked down at the stopwatch she'd kept running on the screen. Their dialogue had so far lasted 2 minute and 19 seconds. It was high time to bail on this link.

Deflated by this exchange, she returned to the VPN to try contacting Jacob again. But Rebecca's attempt to open up the private network only resulted in a Program Error. She tried once more and was confronted with the same dispiriting message. Concerned by this failure, she tried running a diagnostic test on the network, checking its layered protocols and Transport Layer Security. There was no obvious foul-up or glitch that Rebecca could see and yet still the data transfer remained dead to her. Finally, at a loss, she tried restarting her laptop. But still the VPN showed no further signs of life.

It was not a good omen.

Under these circumstances, Rebecca thought it best to switch the laptop off altogether for the time being. She also got up from her seat and turned the lights off in the van. Then she peered out the window, nervously. Taking a leaf out of Jake Brennan's book.

It was dark outside now. Growing darker all the while.

CHAPTER 44

Jacob remained at the table in his cell, glued to the computer screen. Multitasking furiously. His monitor an ever shifting mosaic of windows lighting up, endless data streams, dense cyber traffic. And yet, to his great frustration, he was making little real progress.

Having got inside the Pentagon servers via Radan's trapdoor, Jacob had struggled to make another breakthrough and was no closer to finding what he was looking for. In the meantime another twenty-five minutes had elapsed and the battery life on the laptop continued to ebb, running down in real-time like the meter on a speeding taxi. In truth, Jacob knew he would be lucky if it allowed him another hour's worth of use. And yet still he was stuck on the margins, among the low-level databases. There was nothing here he might show to Cyber Command by way of a serious bargaining chip. Nothing vital enough to stop them in their tracks. Jacob knew he had to somehow get a whole lot deeper.

He was driving at so much more.

Next he tried changing the parameters on SeeR, the Stealth port scanner designed by Radan, and began mapping the system according to these different settings, trying to sniff out points of access. At the same time Jacob brought up a record of the latest software patches applied to the Pentagon operating system, and

pored over these, auditing the fresh additions for
undiscovered bugs. Tell-tale weak-spots that he might
somehow exploit. Any way to get beyond this outer
ring of data and strike at the heart of the operation. The
core of the server where he needed to be.

While Jacob kept running these tasks, the Samsung
phone on the table beeped and vibrated. The one
belonging to Raymond Lowe. Out of interest, Jacob
picked it up and saw that a text message had been sent.
He clicked the message open and read it. How does it
feel to be up shit creek without a paddle?

Then a second message arrived hot on the heels of
the first. Heading in the wrong direction?

Followed by a third. With those dirty brown rapids
carrying you to your doom?

No sooner had Jacob digested this last message than
the dial tone sounded. He let it ring out five times.
Looked at the screen and thought about ignoring this
alert. But in the end, he could not resist the temptation
to have it out with the caller and so Jacob pressed the
green button and held the receiver to his ear.

"Hi pal. How you holding up?"

"That you Chuck?"

"Sure is. Thought I might get hold of you this way.
Only phone still working correctly in the whole of
Grey-3, I took a wild guess it might be in your
possession."

"What is it you want?"

"Just to gloat a little, seeing how things have turned
out. Is that so wrong? Also didn't want you going to
the grave thinking you had the better of me in any way.
Needed to set the record straight on that front."

"So is it the Chinese you're working for?"

"Working with, Jacob. I think that's a better way of
putting it. A spirit of co-operation spanning the Pacific
Rim."

"So you're doing this purely for money?"

"I do love that green stuff, Jacob. Never pretended otherwise. Which is not to say I didn't briefly consider cutting you in. But then you go and prove yourself a cut above the average newbie and that puts me in a very tricky position. You see, I'm getting paid to guarantee certain deficiencies in the overall infrastructure. I have to leave the cat flap open at night for the bad guys to come around and take note. Now how am I going to do that with you acting all vigilant and shit, pulling rabbits out of the hat at every turn? In the end I couldn't trust you to opt for the dark side, Jacob. Had this sneaking suspicion you'd only do the right thing."

"Guess we'll never know now."

"We certainly won't."

"So you pulled this off alone?"

"Not quite. Credit where credit's due. I'm not the only one on the take in the vicinity of PROPS. It did take a little help to put you in the frame like that."

"That include O'Hara. The bloke who filed the report?"

"O'Hara? Sure. The guy's a pro. Dreamt that charge up and then found a way to make it stick. Nice bit of work. I imagine me and him will be teaming up again in the near future. Sorry, Jacob. There's me using the F word again…Anyway, I just want you to know that as far as my own talents go, I was only toying with you. Blowing smoke up your ass. Spent the whole time with one hand tied behind my back in order not to draw attention to myself. I told my oriental colleagues that there was nothing you were capable of that I couldn't do just as well, but they wouldn't have it. Insisted that I take you out of the game."

"That's because they know you were talking crap."

"Is that a fact?"

"So you really think you can live with me technically?"

"Live with you! Take a look around at where you find yourself right now, buddy boy."

"But that has nothing to do with pure programming. It was brought about by you being a two-faced prick."

"'Pure programming'! Listen to yourself! You may have the slight edge on account of those weird dizzy spells, but as for the bigger picture, the wider canvas, I OWN YOU, Jacob. Oh, and talented as you are, you should know it would take you the best part of five hours to trace this phone call, and believe me, five hours is something you don't have at present. Which brings us to the very bad news. Thought I'd give you a heads-up seeing as there's nothing you can do about it now…Fighter squadron is on its way. Looks like you're going out in style with a great big KABBBBOOOOOMMMMM!"

"Is that right…"

"Looking on the bright side, Jacob, you've earned me a fortune. You wouldn't imagine how much it's cost Beijing for me to get you out of the way. Never mind visiting my favourite titty joint – now I'll get to open a string of them from coast to coast!"

"And how are you going to visit them when they'll never let you off base?"

"How? Jesus, Jacob, I'll be in line for a congressional medal after this – helping to bring you down. No more loyal US citizen could you hope to find. Me and President Corrigan chilling in his crib is what I envisage very shortly. After this, I'll be able to come and go as I please."

"What can I say, Chuck. You're one huge arsehole."

"Ouch! Well, so long Jacob. At least the end shouldn't be too painful. Don't think your looking at a lingering death once all them bombs drop on your head."

Jacob said nothing in reply.

"Oh, and one last thing, I see your girlfriend is holidaying in the wilds of Ireland. Heard it's lovely this time of the year, apart from the assembled kill squads dropping out of the sky to spoil the general tranquillity. Her minutes are numbered, Jacob, just like your own. And in case you feel like saying goodbye, I just took your private network down as well. So no chance for the two of you to swap any sucky last words."

"If I ever get out of here, Chuck..."

"I've already explained that to you, champ. It's not going to happen. They're going to bomb you out of existence."

Jacob felt the tremendous urge to curse and rage and give voice to an enormous hatred, but instead he closed the call down, aware that he needed to channel all these feelings in a highly precise way. If he hadn't known it before, then Jacob knew it now. He did not have one more second to lose.

For another twelve minutes, he continued scouring the thousands of ports used by the Pentagon servers, running SYN TCP scans on them. Then, suddenly, a warning box appeared on the screen and Jacob knew that he had company. The Systems Administrator at the Pentagon had logged on to the server and was checking personally for intrusions. Although his heart jumped at this development, Jacob also knew that it presented a real opportunity. If he could somehow access the programmer's own shell then this would allow him to cut to the chase and acquire the same process privileges.

First though, he needed to sow a little confusion.

Jacob brought up another of Radan's programs, this one called aKa, and put it into immediate effect: unleashing a barrage of decoy attacks on the Pentagon server. A thousand perfectly innocent IP addresses, from all over the world, which Radan had already harvested for just such a moment. Every one of them now appeared to be trying to crack the system wide-open. A phantom assault allowing Jacob to hide among their bogus ranks.

Jacob watched as the Administrator started taking frantic counter-measures, running backtraces on the IP addresses, and as he concentrated all his efforts in this direction, Jacob launched a stealth attack on the man's shell, employing a C-String taught to him back at PROPS. The code stripped away at the layered protocols, reverse-engineering a breach in its defences, and as soon as Jacob saw a gap appear, he instantly secured it and entered this very private domain.

Now Jacob injected a kernel module into the systems driver which took hold quickly and began to reconfigure the client system according to his own specific design. As it did so, Jacob checked the battery gauge again and saw that, by its reckoning, he had a total of 1 hour and 52 minutes left. As this number fell by a further seven minutes, Jacob finally gained full access to the internal database machine. He listed the entire Root Menu and then narrowed his search to all those programs beginning with Q.

There were 189 of them in total, but as Jacob studied these frantically, he found that one of them stood out from all its neighbours. It existed as nothing more then a file title and unlike the others there was no sub-directory or associated function on display. Nothing, in fact, except for the file name itself.

Qua/Pro

His heart in his mouth, Jacob ran the program.

There was a wait of twenty long seconds in which nothing appeared to be happening, but then Jacob's screen exploded into life, suddenly dominated by an astonishing flurry of activity. Nothing Radan had

taught him could have prepared Jacob for this moment.
He was staring at a class of algorithm way in advance of
any that had gone before and Jacob knew that nothing
except Quantica could lie beyond it.

The legendary lockbox. The server of myth.

Chapter 45

Rebecca didn't realise she was on the verge of sleep until she snapped awake fully, startled by a sudden concentration of noise. She sat up straight, away from the padded bench, as a second shotgun blast followed the first one and then she heard a sustained burst of automatic fire.

Despite her distance from the combat, it was not difficult to piece together what was going on.

Stuffing the laptop into her rucksack, she felt her way to the entrance of the camper van and opened the door carefully. It was pitch black in the immediate vicinity but she could see several powerful beams of light back towards the cottage, criss-crossing one another. She could also hear shouts from this location as well. Wasting no more time, Rebecca dropped down onto the ground and broke for the dark forest ahead of her. And having reached its edge, she plunged inside.

Heart pounding, adrenalin surging throughout her body, Rebecca pushed onwards. But her passage was far from straight forward, and even as her eyes grew accustomed to the thick gloom, it was still difficult to negotiate the dense foliage which confronted her at every turn. There was no obvious path for Rebecca to keep to, and the tree branches kept sticking out at hostile angles, so that it was all she could do to avoid these wooden barbs. At the same time, she was loath to reduce her speed. And so for five minutes, Rebecca continued at a flat-out pace, risking life and limb, striving to head in a single direction and stay on her feet.

After this time, she stopped for a moment – to catch her breath and check behind her for pursuers. Turning 180 degrees, she could see three separate torch beams off in the distance, although it was impossible to assess how far away they were. The sight of these lights left her feeling even more endangered and so she pressed on immediately and continued with her breathless flight.

A minute later, as Rebecca burst between two beech trees, the ground underfoot fell away. For long panicked moments there was nothing beneath her except thin air, and then, as she landed back on earth, Rebecca stumbled leftwards. At this point a stiff branch caught her in the face, scraping the length of her right cheek. As she reeled from this impact, Rebecca lost her footing altogether. The laptop bag flew off her shoulder before crashing to the forest floor. After several tumbles, she came to a complete stop herself.

Lying flat on her back, looking upwards at the thick canopy of leaves above, she assessed her body for injuries. The worst of it was a sharp pain in her left ankle. Maybe a sprain. "Shit," she muttered under her breath, getting up onto her hands and knees. The laptop bag was on its side, two metres away. Part of her was tempted to leave the machine where it was. After all, there was good reason to think it might be broken. But the stronger instinct was to cling to this possession and maintain a belief in its usefulness.

Rebecca rose to her feet once more, collected the bag. Then she pushed off, testing her damaged ankle. Although it was still possible for her to make progress, this movement was now restricted to an awkward jog.

Adding to this concern, she could hear a helicopter off
in the distance. No doubt it belonged to the armed
search party who were hot on her trail. And in all
likelihood, there'd be a camera on board with the
ability to pick up on the heat signature of her body and
relay her co-ordinates to those pursuing her on foot.

Soon after – with her discomfort growing, and her
ankle starting to giving out – Rebecca reached the far
edge of the tree line and came to a stop. Beyond here
lay a clearing bathed in moonlight. Twenty metres
further on, across the stony ground, she saw a pale
vertical wall rising up for one hundred metres before
it flattened out on top. It was the rockface of an old
abandoned quarry. To scale it entirely was out of the
question, but Rebecca did notice a wide shelf below the
halfway point. To reach it would involve scaling some
thirty metres. It was not an impossible climb, Rebecca
realised, and she was definitely done with running.
There was nothing for it except to try and make for this
elevated shelter.

Her mind made up, she left the protection of the
forest and hobbled towards the foot of the quarry wall.
There Rebecca decided on her first holds and then left
solid ground behind, tiny stones falling away beneath
her feet. Even in the darkness, she could see the blood
dropping onto her t-shirt from the gash in her cheek.
Onto the rocks also, leaving a trail in her wake.

Now Rebecca heard the helicopter again, getter
closer, gaining on her current position. She did not
dare look back over her shoulder, for fear of what she
would see, instead committing every ounce of her
strength to the climb itself. Propelling herself up the
rockface, fighting off the pain in her ankle and her
great bodily fatigue. In this way, after an intense
struggle, Rebecca pulled herself up onto the level
plateau.

Set back into the rockface itself, there was a jagged opening which she scrambled towards. It led into a shallow cove, no more than two metres deep and another two wide, although it was all the shelter she could lay claim to. Limping over to the far end, Rebecca crouched there against the back wall. Then she took out the laptop from her bag and pressed the power button.

Nothing.

"Come on," she said. "Come on." Pressing it again and again. But the button remained completely unresponsive. The damage was lasting and there was nothing more she could do. As Rebecca stared in despair at the defunct screen, the helicopter hove into view, half a mile off, heading her way at speed. Its powerful spotlight sweeping over the treetops, trying to fix Rebecca's position. As it drew ever nearer, she pressed herself against the cave wall, trying to fit her frame into a tight crevice.

First, the copter scoured the length and width of the clearing down below, then it transferred its attentions to the quarry wall, climbing upwards and moving steadily across. Eventually, it drew level with the wide shelf and then a blinding light entered the cave, plumbing its totality. Rebecca froze in response, and did not even dare breath as the beam kept flooding in. After ten dreadful seconds, the light moved off and away.

She had no idea whether or not they had identified her presence, but at least the copter had not stayed there by the quarry wall, training its full glare on her person, and she had to take this as a positive sign. At the same time, Rebecca knew that a positive sign was neither here nor there in the larger scheme of things. At best, she'd bought herself another half hour.

What Rebecca really needed was a miracle.

Chapter 46

With her location confirmed, a British Special Forces unit had been dispatched from the UK to seize Rebecca Kent. Now Zhao Min watched this mission proceed on the large screen of the Operations Room, patched through into their tactical communications system. There were several visual feeds on display, including the image-intensifying goggles of each soldier as they fanned out into the surrounding Irish woodland. Also, centre stage, a relay from the powerful thermal imagining camera on board the Merlin HC3 helicopter which was also in hot pursuit. The unit was working to a grid-like system, clearing each one systematically. At this time there were only two quadrants within a five mile radius of the cottage which were still to be explored.

There had been a casualty early on in the mission. A man in his thirties who had opened fire on the troops from inside the cottage where they believed Kent to be hiding. Zhao had felt an unexpected panic when this fire fight occurred. And a corresponding relief when they stated that the wounded figure was a male.

Now he looked on as the Merlin flew over treetops and reached a clearing beyond the forest. The heat seeking camera trawled across this patch of land and then a tall rockface came into view, and the camera was aimed at this vertical plane, sweeping upwards and along it. At a height of thirty metres, a single wide shelf was identified and then examined in detail. Suddenly, there on the screen, was the tell-tale thermal signature of a human being, crouched towards the rear. "It's a young female," said the camera operator. "Must be the target. At least I don't see who else it could be. Who else would be hiding up there at this time of night? Her co-ordinates are 54°, 13', 48" North. 8°, 13', 27" West."

It was the Commander on the ground who spoke next. "I'm under a mile away. Pull back now."

"How long before you reach her?" Zhao asked from the sidelines, speaking over the Land Digitization Channel.

"Ten minutes tops," came the reply.

It was endgame time for Rebecca Kent. Zhao did not know what the unit's mandate was, and had no control over this situation, but he knew he did not want to see her killed.

Zhao turned to one of the analysts. "Any progress yet with Grey-3?"

"That's a negative. Wylde's measures are holding firm."

"Well unfirm then. We need a breakthrough."

Zhao knew himself to be auditioning for the full time role as Head of PROPS, and that every call he made now would ultimately decide his own fate. There was every chance, should he achieve the right results, that the role was his to keep. Of course, it helped his cause that Kent was in the bag, but this was probably not enough alone to guarantee the promotion. For that to happen, he needed somehow to bring Grey-3 back under control in the half hour still left to him, before the F-16 Falcons blew D Wing to pieces, and Wylde with it. And yet Wylde's coding continued to frustrate all of their counter-measures, despite the furious efforts of all five CIA analysts. Perhaps his best hope,

Zhao reflected, was for Wylde to blow a mental fuse at the eleventh hour.

He had to admit, grudgingly, that the young Englishman was a more than worthy opponent.

Now Zhao looked over at Chuck White as White got up from his chair, stood on his tiptoes, and stretched himself out like a lazy cat. "Nature calls," he announced. Then he strolled across the floor and out of the room, perfectly at his ease, without asking for further permission.

Zhao continued staring at the doorway after White had left.

Half an hour ago, Chuck White was pleading on Kent's behalf. Now, as she stood on the verge of capture, he appeared to be supremely unconcerned about her fate. You might even have thought, looking at him, that everything was falling into place. Especially when Zhao took into account Rebecca Kent's earlier accusation.

There were all kinds of ways of looking at this situation, and each had its pros and cons. But there was no doubting the queasiness Zhao had felt, and felt still, in watching the hunt for Rebecca Kent. It did not sit right with him somehow. Worse still, if it did come to light later – Chuck White's guilt – then it would have happened on his watch, with all that said about his own professional judgement.

Now Zhao muttered something under his breath, and then – as if far from convinced by his own agenda – he got up and followed his colleague out into the corridor. After walking a short way along, Zhao Min entered the men's bathroom – the door still closing on its hinges from when Chuck had passed through.

CHAPTER 47

For the first few minutes Jacob marvelled at the astonishing vision displayed on his computer screen. At the same time, he was also trying to take a reading of it as well. Hoping, in this way, to come to terms with this radical encryption technique and feel his way into its complex architecture.

What confronted him was a swirling matrix of numbers. There were thousands upon thousands of them in perpetual motion. Both a loose arrangement and a binding structure. It was like a real-time simulation of a tornado containing several distinct vortices, every one of which obeyed its own hidden rules, only adding to the vast complexity of the whole.

Underneath this weird, rotating column of figures, at the very bottom of the screen, were nine separate boxes for data entry. Jacob knew that he had to subtract this exact number, in their correct sequence, from the maelstrom in view. It was a form of visual cryptography with no fixed points. The burning question was how this might be achieved. Nothing in Radan's suite of software was going to be any help in this endeavour. Jacob accepted there was nothing for it except to look deep inside himself and explore the hidden limits.

At the same time, in the back of his mind, lay the issue of Rebecca's personal safety. A painful distraction which was trying to take him over. However, Jacob knew it was essential to put her out of his mind and simply pray that she could hold out on her own. Stay one step ahead of the hunting pack. Yes, he was probably in a position to mess with the Comms channels of that military unit sent to seize her, and sever their satellite link-ups, but all this would lead to was a short delay.

Unless Jacob penetrated Quantica, they were both as good as dead.

Focus, he told himself. Somewhere inside this seething pattern lay a set of attracting forces. It was all about searching out the recurring patterns, the inescapable symmetries, and then withdrawing these core components from the rolling design.

Jacob stared at the screen so long and hard that his vision blurred and he had to blink his eyes back into focus. But still he dared not look away or break with his concentration, even as he felt it provoke in him a growing sense of inner-turbulence. These were the same warning signals which had led to his seizure back at PROPS, and Jacob could sense the same accelerating dangers. And yet he also knew that he needed to give himself over to this powerful force if he was going to succeed.

As this turbulence increased, Jacob's peripheral vision began to fade out and his sense of self went tumbling away. Once again, he was straddling the border between wakefulness and dreams. Both the source of his mental powers and the site of his greatest fears. But Jacob knew he had no option except to embrace this mindset, whatever the cost. There was no other way for him to reach through to Quantica without it.

As the trance state took him over, Jacob's view of the shape-shifting logarithms also underwent a deep change. While they still existed as numbers, there was also an aura attached to their complex movements. An inner resonance. Enabling to Jacob sift through this data as if tuning into a frequency, casting off static all the while. He knew that he was looking for the prime movers in their midst, and that all the other numbers were mere emanations of these nine, there to cloud the truth and confuse his understanding. The fundamental structure was only to be had if he kept on searching and surrendered to the process.

It was now that Jacob started to experience an onrush of exhilaration as he began to channel these insights. This was what he was born to do. His way of shining brightly. Tearing up all these digital veils. And as he continued to experience this wild delight, three numbers leap to the fore:

2-4-1

It was as if they were suddenly present for Jacob in three dimensions, unlike the rest of the combined mass. He recognised them as one entity, distinct from those thousands of floating point operations all round, and as his eyes continued to follow their spinning orbits, they refused to surrender this glaring singularity. And so, convinced of their uniqueness, he typed these numbers into the first three boxes below.

The tornado-like structure responded to Jacob's opening selection as if stung into action by it. Now the several columns began to rotate at even greater speed. A raging vortex of calculus. But far from being concerned by this increase, Jacob kept to his task with burning intensity, looking to cut through the torrent of numbers and divine the integral code within. After another minute – of which he was hardly aware – another trio of digits rose to prominence with absolute clarity. 8-6-7. Jacob followed them and followed them and still their relevance did not diminish. Like flashing gold particles caught up in the eye of the storm, they struck him with revelatory force, and so Jacob typed in these three digits as well.

Now the vortex responded again to this further intrusion. The motion and violence of the structure reaching tremendous heights. Taken together, it resembled a wounded hive, spewing out bees in order to protect the Queen. Striking out blindly, with nothing left to lose. And yet Jacob could not allow himself to be deflected by this roiling mayhem. Instead he needed to find the remnants of order in it. The final link in the chain.

In so doing, Jacob had moved beyond his earlier exuberance. Now it felt as if his mind was on fire. Torched by this storm of calculations. He had reached the point where he was able to penetrate this convulsion of data at the fractal level. Sensing that which lay behind everything. The language of life itself…

3-0-2

As the trio of numbers whirled around, Jacob could still perceive the lines between them, even at the lightning speeds at which they now travelled. He had their true measure. They shone like stars in the night sky. An unmoving constellation.

Jacob typed these three numbers into the last of the boxes, and then, as the numerical firestorm began to implode, he was no longer present to witness the results, having lost regular consciousness. Again he had passed on and and entered that realm beyond where the recurring vision awaited him. A chain of numbers spiralling away through the vast black emptiness of space like a blazing thread of rope. But this time, Jacob could not keep his distance from the awesome spectacle. As if he was a captive of its gravitational pull, he found himself coming closer, closer still, until he had made contact with its wave-like surface and then fused with the structure as a whole.

Now there was nothing to see except a pulsating pearl-grey light, an all-encompassing strobe effect which enveloped his entire being. What Jacob felt, most of all, was a profound sense of belonging here. And because of this, the great temptation to bask in this stream of light until he was fully integrated. All that prevented him from doing so was a lingering sense of unease. Vague but nonetheless insistent. And in order to rediscover the reasons for this unease, Jacob knew it would be necessary to disentangle himself from this energy source and recall the particulars.

As he strove to do this, the first flashback hit him. It showed his mother on Formby beach, standing above Jacob's younger self, drying his hair with a towel. Then this image cut out and Jacob saw himself walking home from school alone, cutting through Wavertree Park on an autumn day, the leaves scuttling along at his feet. Then the action jumped forward to PROPS, and he was sitting in the canteen, staring over at Rebecca, desperate to introduce himself. After that, a snapshot of his father standing in the hallway of their house, a tartan suitcase in his hand. He shook his head sadly and smiled down at his seven year old son. The front door was open already and there was a black hackney cab waiting outside.

Still these random visuals continued, as if Jacob's entire existence was on shuffle: a flicker book of images playing at explosive speeds, with enormous vividness.

The unfinished business of his life.

When Jacob came to, he was on the floor of the cell, curled up on his side. He struggled to his feet, held on to the desk, and stared at the clock in the corner of the laptop's screen. It had only been five minutes, he estimated, since he'd lost consciousness, although it felt like a lifetime ago. Seized by a wave of nausea, Jacob rushed over to the toilet bowl and was violently sick inside of it. At the same time, the left side of his head lit up with an intense burst of pain. He ran the tap and threw a little cold water into his face, but that was the only relief Jacob allowed himself. There was still no time to lose…

Returning to the table, Jacob saw, to his incredible relief, that the contents of the Quantica server were there on open display. He counted a mere nineteen files, but surely these were of the utmost importance, given the defences erected around them. Certainly that was his undying hope. Fearing their sudden withdrawal, Jacob did not inspect the contents in detail. Instead he sat down, fought off his physical and mental weakness, and began downloading the entire directory. Then he replicated these files before securing them in several different online locations. At the same time that he did this, Jacob copied the file names and pasted these titles into a Word document.

It was time to share what he'd learnt with the people in power.

CHAPTER 48

Chuck White was stood in front of a urinal when Zhao Min entered the bathroom and leant against one of the wash basins. At this, White turned half way round. "What is it, Zhao? Your hormones acting up as well? You thinking of taking the big step and resorting to man-love? Sorry, brother, think I'm going to hold out a while longer yet…"

"I think you believe that you don't have much longer to wait," Zhao answered. "And this is because soon you expect to be living in your own playboy mansion paid for by the People's Republic of China."

White – betraying no sign of upset – zipped himself up and turned to face his accuser. "That is some crazy-ass speculation, Zhao. What is this, improv night? You playing up to the cameras?" He gestured up at the security feed in the corner of the ceiling.

"There are no cameras operating in here at present, White," Zhao replied, "because I had no wish for them to hear what I am about to say. This speculation of mine is not speculation at all. It is fact. I have always had my suspicions about you, which is why I have spent a great many hours of late reviewing the charges against Jacob Wylde. Your problem is that for all your flashes of intuition, you're ultimately blinded by your own egotism. And so you cannot fight the temptation to let people know just how clever you are. That, I think, is why I was able to find your fingerprints still there at the crime scene. It was not Wylde who conspired with a foreign government. It was you."

Chuck shook his head repeatedly. "Bullshit."

"No. As I've told you, this is the truth."

"For one thing, there's no way you'd have taken time out from our current mission brief to launch this dramatic exposé. No way that Graves would have stood for it either."

"I think you underestimate how much I despise you."

Now the breezy defiance fell away slightly and a noticeable hardness set in to Chuck's features. He spread his feet a little further apart, looked at the tiled floor, then back up at Zhao. "And yet, you haven't gone to anybody with this ridiculous accusation of yours, otherwise I'd be in chains right now."

"That is also true."

"So what's you're line of thinking?"

"I have a proposition for you, White."

Chuck White stood still by way of reply. Said nothing.

"I said I have a proposition."

"I'm listening," he answered reluctantly.

"If you will agree to turn double agent for the US government then I can guarantee you a full pardon, plus an impressive salary as well. Maybe not up to the pay-scale offered by your Chinese masters, but under the circumstances, not bad at all."

Chuck laughed, pinched his nose. "I don't see how you'd be in a position to guarantee any such thing. Last time I looked you weren't the President of this country."

"No. But the logic is clear. In Wylde we have the villain of the piece. Not to mention an ongoing security threat, regardless of the rights and wrongs. After he's been taken out, there isn't going to be so much of an appetite for another execution. Not when they discover that they've made a terrible mistake."

"So you're proposing he still gets whacked?"

"That is correct. If we have ourselves an agreement then I conveniently say nothing until tomorrow afternoon. Then, of course, I get to bring you in myself."

"Sheriff Zhao to the rescue."

"Exactly. And then I argue the case for clemency as well. Tell them how invaluable you would prove as an asset."

Chuck raised his left hand to his face; rubbed his chin with the flat of his palm. "Or else I could slam your head against the wall, repeatedly, and leave you for dead."

"True, but it's going to take a lot of explaining. And when they retrieve my laptop and sift through it, it's going to tell a very different story to the one which you would have them believe."

Chuck nodded, thinking this through, and walked over to the sink to Zhao's left. He ran the water, added soap from the dispenser, worked up a lather, rinsed that soap off. Then he took out four paper towels, dried his hands thoroughly with these and tossed them into the bin to his right. Finally he turned and stepped towards Zhao, extending his right hand. "Ok, Zhao, all things considered, you've got yourself a deal."

The two men shook on it. White looked pale and downcast for once. He was far from happy, but the decision had been taken.

Chuck White left the bathroom first. Zhao Min stayed as he was for several moments. Then he turned and looked at himself in one of the mirrors. After that, he made the phone call.

By the time Zhao Min returned to The Operations Room, Chuck White was sat down already, staring intently at his monitor. As Zhao walked down the steps leading to the large semi-circular table, two military guards rushed past him, pistols drawn, shouting instructions. "Get on the floor and lie face down! Now!" These instructions were clearly aimed at Chuck White.

Faced with this intervention, Chuck shot up from his chair. "What the hell, Zhao?"

But he did not stay that way for long as both soldiers were already forcing him onto his knees and then his stomach. "The floor, White. Now!"

Zhao walked over to Chuck, and leaned over him, as his arms were pulled back rudely and the cuffs were applied. "The funny thing is that I had nothing on you, White. Not a single shred of evidence…I think we can say with certainty that the joke is on you." Then he raised himself back up and turned to one of the analysts. "Get me Graves now."

CHAPTER 49

Back in the Secure Conferencing Area, Zhao Min addressed his superiors in Washington, the same grouping as before.

"A grave error has occurred," Zhao informed them. "It is clear now that Jacob Wylde had nothing to do with the Chinese Government. This was all the doing of Chuck White."

It took a few moments for the bombshell to sink in.

"You're absolutely sure?" Purdy asked.

"100%. There can be no further doubt."

The Defence Secretary paused, bit into his bottom lip. "I see. Well, thank you for bringing this to our attention, Zhao. I'll expect a preliminary report on this shortly."

"Of course, sir. I will make it a priority."

"I would ask now that you allow us the opportunity to consider this development in private."

"Yes. Of course."

As the link with Zhao went dead, Purdy swivelled his chair around to face both colleagues. "Well I guess that turns things right on their heads."

General Barnes was first to respond. "OK, this may clear his name, but does it make Wylde any less of a security threat? It's a question worth asking, I think, before we stand this mission down. It seems as if there's no controlling this individual. I still believe the peace of mind this action would allow us outweighs the obvious costs."

Purdy nodded at this. "Admittedly, it's a valid concern. Charles, what's your take on this?"

"I think it's a call that only the President himself can make," Graves replied.

Purdy nodded, leant forward, and pressed a button on his phone – contacting the President's chief aide, over in Moscow. "What's the hold up, Peters? Surely the meeting with Sologub should be breaking up by now."

"They're wrapping up the photo-op this moment," Peters answered. "The President will be with you in two minutes, sir."

Purdy turned to General Barnes. "And how long before the F-16s reach Grey-3?"

"ETA is fifteen minutes," the General replied.

Thirty seconds later, President Corrigan finally came on the line and addressed Purdy directly. "What's the latest, Bob?" he asked.

"Mr President, we continue to face a highly challenging situation. Although it is one which has changed radically in the last five minutes."

"Ok. Let's hear it then…"

It was as Purdy began his delivery of the facts, that the audio connection went down. To be replaced by a loud, high-pitched tone which had all three men wincing. Then, as this sound ceased abruptly, a different voice altogether could be heard over the line. "This is Jacob Wylde. You can all hear me?" The connection was weak, but audible all the same.

It was Purdy who answered, hardly skipping a beat, in spite of the shocking intrusion. "We can, Mr Wylde. You're talking with Secretary of Defence Purdy, General Barnes, and Charles Graves, who you already know."

"I'm very close to losing power so I'll keep this short. I just caught the last of your little debate and decided I'd weigh in on the subject, just in case you made up your minds to blow this place up all the same. Thought you'd better know the kind of insurance I have in place."

"Go on."

"I've cracked the Quantica server wide open. The one that doesn't exist according to your man Graves. I've got a rundown here of the contents…Shrike, Cull-Wrap, X2-Y40…These ringing any bells?"

Purdy looked over at Charles Graves and he nodded back, grimly.

"So what now?" Purdy asked.

"Anything happens to me or Rebecca Kent and these all become open source and enter the public domain. Believe me, it'll make Project Eames look like a picnic."

"You must know that we had not made the decision to harm you, Jacob. We were simply considering all available options, as we always do in these cases."

"Fine. Good. Great. Just thought I'd make your job that little bit easier. Nothing happens to either of us. And you call your troops off Rebecca Kent now."

Purdy turned to the General."Make the call."

"You better pray nothing has happened to her already," Jacob added, "or else this all gets a whole lot less friendly."

Within seconds General Barnes had got through to the British Command Centre. "Wilkins. This is General Barnes. Have your men made contact with the target yet?…Then stand them down now. I repeat stand down Tango-Brave now…" He nodded over at Purdy.

"OK. It's done. She's safe now," Purdy said.

But Jacob had no chance to comment on this development, for that was the moment when the battery on his laptop finally gave out. He looked at the screen as its light ceased abruptly and all he could see therein was a dim reflection of himself. Jacob slumped back against his chair, surrendering to extreme fatigue. Off in the distance he heard the low rumble of aircraft approaching the island. Louder and louder, until they were directly overhead. Then they were moving beyond it, ever more distant.

Game Over.

With one last push, Jacob dragged himself over to the bunk and fell down against the hard mattress, collapsing through total exhaustion. This time nothing awaited him except a dark dreamless sleep.

Chapter 50

It was three days before Jacob could stay awake long enough to take his bearings properly. Until then he'd been slipping in and out of consciousness ever since they'd wheeled him out of D1/Y. Now he realised that he'd been transferred up to one of the medical bays at Grey-3. His head felt sore and cloudy and every inch of his body ached. Propping himself up on both elbows, Jacob considered his immediate surroundings and saw that he was hooked up to a bank of monitors, with pads attached to his wrists, his chest, both temples. It was not a pleasant surprise, reminding him as it did of those earlier examinations which had taken place not so far away. As Jacob started to detach himself from every one of these implements, a doctor came rushing in.

"Please! You need to stop that!"

But instead of complying, Jacob only climbed down from the bed, struggled to his feet, and stared down at the green smock covering his naked body. "Get me some regular clothes to put on, will you. And I want Stanley Watson in here as well. Me and him need to talk." Then Jacob walked over to the corner and sat down gingerly in the room's only chair.

The doctor hesitated. Then he went back outside. This was a relief to Jacob as it seemed to indicate that his threat held good, meaning that Cyber Command were not confident of having retrieved all the copies of the Quantica server while he was still out cold. But then, Jacob reasoned, there was no way for them to know for sure just how many copies he'd made. And for that reason, there was a need for his opponents to tread carefully right now. Certainly, given the doctor's obedient response, Jacob appeared to be the one who was holding straight aces.

There was nothing joky about Watson's conduct this time around as he entered the room, ten minutes later. Instead he acted like the two of them had never met before.

Jacob didn't bother with any preamble. "Rebecca Kent. Where is she now?"

"I understand she's still in Ireland."

"And why's that?"

"On account of a friend in hospital who was badly injured in an incident over there."

"An incident…"

"Yes. That's all I know."

"But she's OK?"

"I understand she's fine. Yes."

"OK. Well you need to get me off this rock now and back over to the states. I've got some urgent business with Cyber Command."

"It would be best for you to stay here a couple more days, Jacob. Simply to rest up."

"No way."

Watson nodded. "All right then. If that's how you feel about it, I'll see what I can do."

"You do that," Jacob answered.

∗

The C-130 Hercules arrived next morning and the flight took off soon after with Jacob Wylde on board. This time he was flown to the city of Johannesburg, the nearest major city on the map, and from there transferred onto an unmarked Lear jet leaving for

Washington DC. Apart from himself, there was no one else present on this second plane but the flight crew, and a single young man, dressed like an office clerk, who served Jacob food twice. Outside of these mealtimes, Jacob continued to drift in and out of sleep, his body and mind still far from restored.

After twelve hours in the air, they landed on one of the outer runways at Dulles International instead of gracing any local military facility. This certainly felt like progress. Jacob was left to disembark the aircraft alone and met by a chauffeured Lincoln MKT at the foot of the steps. He climbed in the back and was driven directly to The Four Seasons Hotel on Penn Ave. It was only as the car pulled up outside that the driver turned and addressed him. "Just give them your name at the desk. I'll be back to pick you up tomorrow morning. Ten sharp."

"OK. Fine."

Jacob checked into a room on the 14th floor. The king size bed was the first thing in there to tempt him, but he tried delaying his next siesta, opting for a long soak in the bath instead. Afterwards he watched television distractedly for a couple hours. And then, once more, succumbed to tiredness.

It was only in the early evening, after dinner in his room, that Jacob tried ringing his mother (he had delayed the call a couple of times on account of the anxiety he felt, not knowing what to expect). The phone rang out several times, followed by the beep of an answering machine. It was only as Jacob started to leave a message, that his mother picked up, alerted by the sound of her son's voice.

"Jacob?!"

"Hiya, Ma. How's it going?"

"Jesus! You're still alive! I haven't known what to

think or do with myself. The last few months have been a nightmare."

"I know, but don't worry. The worst of it is over."

"They've let you go?"

"Something like that. Listen, I've still got a few things to take care of first, and I'm not sure exactly how long this'll take, but I'll be back to see you within the month."

"But you'll be in touch again before then?"

"Of course, I'll give you a call again in a couple of days when I'm feeling more together. This is just to let you know I'm basically all right."

"You sound shattered."

"I am. I'll tell you all about it soon."

CHAPTER 51

Next morning, Jacob sensed an improvement in his overall condition. Mentally and physically, it felt like he was now beginning to mend. After a light breakfast of coffee and toast, he headed out into the August sunlight at five minutes before the scheduled hour. Across from The Four Seasons, the driver from yesterday was already tucked into the curbside. Jacob walked straight over and climbed into the back of the Lincoln. Again he found himself unaccompanied, with no authority figure issuing orders for Jacob to follow. It was a kind of solitude he greatly enjoyed.

To Jacob's surprise, he was not brought to a stop outside any official government building. Instead they drove the short distance to a large, newly built business complex on M Street. Here the driver parked up, got out of the car, encouraged Jacob to do the same. Then he escorted him inside the main entrance and over to the general reception desk. The driver handed over an ID card to the man on duty, and after this was processed, the man issued two security passes.

An elevator took them up to the 24th floor. It opened out onto an expensive-looking foyer which might have belonged to a leading law firm; but there was no sign to indicate its function. And although a receptionist was stood behind the front desk, she failed to raise her head and acknowledge their arrival. In fact, she made a deliberate point of not looking their way.

"Go straight through," said the driver, gesturing to a corridor off to the right. "You want 5A."

Jacob nodded, passed beyond the reception area, and into a plushly carpeted hallway. He counted off the room numbers until he was stood outside the correct one, and then he entered. Inside lay a small conference suite with the lights on and the blinds pulled down. A bald, bespectacled man was already waiting for him there and gestured to the chair opposite his own, across a dark wood table. "Please, take a seat."

Jacob did as he was asked and sat back in the chair.

"Good morning, Mr Wylde. My name is Devin Chambers and you should know that I am fully authorised to speak on behalf of the United States Government as we seek to reach a settlement which is satisfactory to both parties."

"That's all very good, but I want to have this out with Graves."

"Graves?"

"Cut the crap. You know who he is. And I'm going nowhere until I speak with him. Charles Graves is the one who started the ball rolling and so he can be the one to bring it to a stop."

Chambers stared at him. "Well, I don't know that Mr Graves is available at present, but I will look into it for you, if that's what you want."

"Good. I'd ask that you do that now."

Chambers went out of the room to make the call and then returned five minutes later. This time, he only stuck his head around the door. "Mr Graves will be here in precisely one hour."

They brought Jacob a coffee while he waited and he drank it slowly. In truth, it was not an unpleasant delay. Time to reflect on what he wanted to say, and his reasons for saying these things. Time to think back on the last couple of months. Also, it was pleasing to know that the head of Cyber Command was being forced to alter his schedule – obliged to go out of his way.

When Graves walked in, sixty minutes later, he sat down without ceremony. "You wanted to see me," he said in a voice which was cold and flat, with an expression to go with it.

"Yeh. I thought it best if we met face to face."

"Well, as I understand it, Mr Chambers already had the authority to make this deal."

"That's all very well, but I'd prefer to deal with you."

"Ok, Wylde. Here I am. As requested. What is it you want?"

"I'll start with the obvious. Nothing happens to myself or Rebecca from here on out. We get to disappear. Enjoy an early retirement. Stop looking over our shoulders from the word go."

"Of course. That is only to be expected"

"Also the money to achieve this. Two million dollars. Not a bad price, all things considered, given that we've outed a major Chinese spy."

"And continue to blackmail the US government…"

"Call it any way you like. You know the situation here."

Graves leant down and lifted his briefcase onto the table. He opened it, took out two Manila envelopes and passed these across the table. "We have already taken the precaution of opening bank accounts in both your names. Now I will see to it that those sums of money are transferred to them before the end of the day. There is also a new British passport for you in there."

"Good. And Rebecca – is she still in Ireland?

"As of this morning, she was. At The Gresham Hotel. She's been visiting Jake Brennan in hospital this last week."

"And who's Jake Brennan?"

"On old comrade of hers."

"What's wrong with him?"

"Recovering from a couple of bullet wounds. Although, as I understand it, he's expected to make a full recovery."

"You better hope so, because otherwise that's on you as well. You've got the address of that hotel where Rebecca's staying?"

"Of course." Graves took a card from his jacket pocket and slid it across the table.

"What about Professor Radan?" Jacob asked.

Graves stared back at him. "It gives me no pleasure to inform you that Farid Radan is dead. Needless to say, those responsible will be made accountable for their actions. In fact, a tribunal is already being set up with this task in mind."

"It was that bastard, Havers, wasn't it?"

"I believe Havers is one of those helping us with our investigation, yes. But let's not pretend that you are entirely without blame in all these matters. That would be to stretch the truth to breaking point. The fact is this all started because you committed a very serious crime."

"I'm not pretending otherwise, Graves. But it's also true that you broke all kinds of international laws to bring me over here. Same thing again when I was framed by Chuck White. Nothing but on-the-spot judgements all the way. I could also include the very real possibility that your president was on the verge of having me killed without good cause."

"I'm confident it wouldn't have come to that."

"Yeah? Well that makes you a whole lot more confident than me."

Graves leaned forward in his seat and rested his forearms on the table. "I know you think we're the bad guys, Wylde, but that only goes to show your own ignorance of things. We do what we do in order to face down ugly threats of a terrible magnitude. Day after day after day."

"I'm not saying that you don't. All I know is that I want out of the whole business. Me and Rebecca both. With enough money for us to walk away."

"And do you think of this as money owing to you?" Graves asked.

"After everything that's gone on, I can't say that's a question which troubles me a great deal."

Graves nodded at this answer, narrowed his steely blue eyes.

"And what happens now to Chuck White?" Jacob asked.

"A straight trade. He gets your old room in Grey-3."

"Not much for him to laugh about down there," Jacob said.

"No. I don't suppose there is..." Graves answered. "Now there is one question we need to put to you. Not a pleasant one, but important all the same. What if some accident should befall you in future? One which looked suspicious, but wasn't in truth. Even you, as far as I can tell, are not beyond these kinds of freak occurrences."

"In that case I'd leave it up to Rebecca to make the decision. I'm sure she'd be able to call it the right way."

"OK, fine, but what if something should happen to the pair of you? And understand, this is not a threat."

Jacob shrugged his shoulders. "In that case, I guess you're screwed."

"That's how it is?"

"I'd say so."

Graves nodded, stared long and hard at Jacob. "Is that everything then?"

"Yep. I think that's me and you done."

Immediately, Graves got up from his seat. "You'll understand if I don't offer you my hand."

"Not to worry. I'm sure I'll get over it."

Happily, when Jacob got back to The Four Season Hotel, there was no need to ring Dublin. A message was already waiting for him at reception.

Meet me at Dulles airport at 3.35pm. I'm due in on Flight AA810. Let's take it from there.

R

xx

CHAPTER 52

An hour later, Jacob was stood inside the arrivals lounge at Dulles International Airport. According to the board, there was no delay on her flight, and it was due to land in the next half hour. He had butterflies in his stomach at the thought of seeing Rebecca again, and the minutes of his wait flew by as Jacob thought about things to say to her and then just as soon wrote them off.

At the scheduled time, Rebecca was one of the first through the gate and she picked Jacob out instantly from the expectant crowd. She was wearing faded jeans, an old denim jacket, and had nothing more than a small beige leather bag over one shoulder by way of luggage. She also looked a little tired, but beautiful as ever as far as Jacob was concerned. He came forward to meet her, and they stood inches apart, both hesitating for a moment. Then Rebecca smiled and dispelled the awkwardness by planting a full kiss on Jacob's mouth. After the kiss, she pulled back and stared into his face. "You look like how I feel."

"I could say the same thing about you," he answered. And yet it was obvious that, for all her weariness, Rebecca was riding a crest of a wave, just like himself.

They were both hopped up on freedom.

"I suggest we both get gone from the US," she announced.

"You're serious?"

"Definitely. I'm all in favour of a quick turnaround. All these air miles we've been accruing, I reckon we're in line for a couple of free flights."

"I don't think we need to worry too much about air miles," Jacob answered.

"Is that so?"

"Yes it is. I just negotiated us a retirement package."

"Well aren't you just the man of the hour. Wonder if it's anywhere close to the figure I had in mind."

"I'd certainly hope so."

"So would I. OK, let's grab a coffee and then we can decide what we're going to do."

They walked a short way off, stopped at a Cinnabon café, and chose a table from where the departures board could be viewed. Jacob was served at the counter, and while carrying back two macchiattos, he saw that Rebecca was studying the list of flights intently.

"You sure you haven't had enough of air travel for one day?" he said.

"Not a bit of it. I'm ready to go again. Got me a brand new passport which needs its first foreign stamp."

"This one got your own name in?" Jacob asked.

Rebecca laughed.

After Jacob had sat down, he took out a Manila envelope from his inside jacket pocket and pushed it across the table. "I believe this is yours." She looked at the brown wrapper for a second, then Rebecca opened it calmly and held up the paper with the bank details on it.

"Should be a million dollars inside of that account by the end of the day," Jacob added.

Rebecca looked up at him. "So you asked for seven figures each?"

"I though that was only fair."

She nodded, smiled, looked back inside the envelope

and located a debit card down at the envelope's bottom. This Rebecca pocketed. "So you've got your passport with you as well?"

Jacob removed it from his jacket and waved it around.

Then a thought occurred to Rebecca and suddenly her features darkened. "And what about Radan?"

"Not good news…"

"He'd dead, isn't he?"

"How did you know?"

"Going on the last time I saw him, It wasn't so hard to foresee. I wouldn't say that he was welcoming the grim reaper home, but he certainly wasn't fleeing its clutches either."

"He's the only reason we're both sitting here today, I guess."

"And then some. Without the professor we'd both have been finished. I think we need to find a way to honour his memory."

"Amen to that."

"And you've spoken with your mother?" Rebecca asked.

"Last night."

"And she's OK?"

"She's good. Told her I'd be back within the month to check on things."

"Which leave us with thirty days to get to know one another a little better."

Jacob laughed and gestured to the board. "Well go ahead. Take your pick. Anywhere in particular in mind?""

"How about St Lucia?"

"Sounds good."

"I saw a program on it once. Looks like a pretty quiet island," Rebecca said.

"Quiet works for me right now. Although no more ten pm curfews."

"Nope," said Rebecca. "I wouldn't have thought so. Although I do have a few ground rules of my own which you'll need to learn."

"So it's like that," Jacob smiled.

"I don't know what it's like," Rebecca smiled back. "But I guess we're going to find out."

******

Kuba - A Rogue
Hackers Freebie

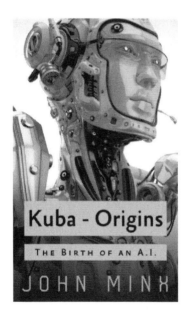

The Troubled Birth of a Super Powerful A.I...

This ten thousand word short focuses on Kuba – the
A.I from Books 2 and 3 in the Rogue Hackers Series
– plunging us into the murky world of Moscow as the
Soviet State Collapses, when a brilliant mathematician

rewrites the rules of what is possible with artificial intelligence, and his stunning creation catches the attention of the Russian mob...

To grab a free digital copy, please check with your online retailer of choice.

Deep Spiral - Rogue Hackers Book 2

After a brief rest on a tropical island, Jacob and
Becca set out on a fact finding mission to the Amazon
jungle, accepting an invite from Russian Tech
Billionaire, Krystof Rogozin. But it's a tropical journey
which soon spins out of control, setting in motion a

runaway drama. One which unearths the facts about Jacob's true identity, even as it forces him to make use of his strange powers like never before.

With the action moving from the North of Brazil to the city of Berlin, all is not what it seems, and Jacob must navigate his path through a landscape of smoke and mirrors as he copes with more than one master of deceit. The stakes rising by the second before reaching their climax in the high mountains of Kazakhstan, where the young man's destiny at last becomes doubtless, with huge implications for Planet Earth as a whole.

DARK PILGRIM - ROGUE HACKERS BOOK 3

Assassinate His Girlfriend or Surrender The World!

The third installment in The Rogue Hackers Series, featuring even more high drama, alien contact, psychic warfare, and mind-blowing tech.

With his mind in pieces, and his spirit broken, Jacob Wylde has never been in greater need of those amazing cosmic powers encoded in his DNA. Aware that these, and these alone, might free his girlfriend from the clutches of the alien invader that has taken Rebecca Kent for its host.

At the same time, all around him, voices are arguing that he must write her off as dead and buried for the sake of humanity. Patching Jacob up for a suicide mission as The Dark Pilgrim readies itself to deliver a momentous speech at the United Nations. Offering the forces of resistance this one last chance to alter the course of world history and foil the alien's earth-shattering masterplan.

And so, with the clock ticking down on apocalypse, Jacob is faced with the most disturbing of choices – either give his all to freeing Becca or train his mind on blowing her away . . .

A question that haunts his every step, even as the world teeters on the brink of destruction and the ruling global order starts to unravel. Setting the scene for an epic confrontation between the two civilizations and its champions of darkness and light. A new high point for The Rogue Hackers Series, Dark Pilgrim is an action packed book brimming with perilous intrigue, and heart-stopping moments of high drama, offering the reader thrills galore.

Printed in Great Britain
by Amazon